CHATTEL ROYALE: OZ

Also by Howard Gardos

The Bethesda Wars (available on Kindle)

Branches
The Short Life and Death of Little Frankie Morris
Roberta's Story
Confrontation
Shadowman
Lost Shadow
Face Off
The Tanks
Little Girls
The Apostle
Twins
True Stories
Fathers
Bad Dreams
The Blue Van

Available on Kindle and paperback:

Did All the Animals on Noah's Ark Get Along?
The Extraordinarily Lucky Day in the Unlucky Life of David Pryce
The Guide

The Achilles Trilogy
Achille's Heel
Siren's Song
Odyssey
IV

Chattel Royale: Oz

Howard Gardos

If you took this book to read to a young child or give to a young child put it the fuck back.

For Jill and Neil and Jeremy and Corey and Adam…but especially Corey and Adam, because they were drawn to the messed up shit at a young age, too.

WHEN DOROTHY GALE WAS

GROWING UP in the farmlands of Kansas she never thought she would find herself fighting a lion to the death. And she never thought that particular lion would be one of her closest friends, and that in the background another close friend would be screaming in agony. But that was exactly where she was.

The blade in her hand was light and sharp, and she swung it toward the lion's eyes, hoping to blind him.

"*Stand back Lion*," she shouted, thrusting the blade back and forth, at one point trimming several whiskers.

A low rumble built in the back of Lion's throat. He was soaked in blood, though much of it was not his own. The Tin Woodman (born as Nick Chopper but known to all now as the Tin Woodman) had gotten one good whack in with his axe before disappearing back into the forest, but the wound had not gone deep.

The majority of the blood belonged to his companion and lover, the Hungry Tiger. When they had awakened to find they had been kidnapped to the reproduction of Oz they had been the least upset of their companions by their imprisonment; they were together, and that was all that mattered. Their deep friendship had matured and they would have been happy to live here indefinitely. But then their world was chosen for culling.

Lion had had already taken the hit on his hindquarters from the Tin Woodman (his tin clanging as he disappeared back into the underbrush) when he came upon his love.

The Hungry Tiger was shaking in what Lion took to be fear, but he quickly saw it was something altogether different. Tiger had disappeared into a primal state of gluttony. Ripped to shreds at his paws was Glinda, the Good Witch of the South. Tiger was feasting on her innards.

The Hungry Tiger turned, several links of Glinda's intestines hanging from his mouth. His eyes met with Lion's.

Tiger's eyes filled with tears. Sausage guts spilled forth from his tremendous mouth.

I am no longer hungry, he announced. He lifted his bloodied snout, exposing his bare throat. *Please make it quick, my love.*

Lion stepped forward and placed his huge head against his lover's. He let the Hungry Tiger lose a moment in his mane.

Lion then ripped the Hungry Tiger's throat out in one giant bite. Tiger stiffened for a moment, a deluge of blood drenching Lion's upper half. Then, with a look of acceptance, the Hungry Tiger fell limp to the ground.

No Lion moaned, thinking of the last time they had lay together, how he had stuck his claws into the side of Tiger when penetrating from behind, the Hungry Tiger not hungry then either, rather roaring in pleasure and pain.

Just then he heard the wild, agonized scream of his old friend the Scarecrow.

NO, Lion said, and then roared, so loudly the trees shook and small birds disappeared into the sky. He stood over his lover's body, snarling and roaring. Then, on the other side of a small valley, he heard rustling.

Overcome with blind fury, he moved quickly, leaving the forest. He ran through a small shallow pond, and on the other side he found the girl, wearing thick leather armor, holding a blade in her hand.

A part of him knew it was not just a 'girl', but Dorothy Gale, a dear dear friend who he would have quite willingly sacrificed his life for, at other times.

"*Stand back Lion*," she shouted, lunging with her sharpened blade. She hoped to land a crippling blow before the much larger beast could attack but she just managed to clip some of his thick, blood soaked whiskers.

Lion paced before her, his eyes burning with primal rage, a deep growl building in his throat.

Dorothy sensed she did not have the upper hand. The armor she wore might withstand an initial assault but looking at the huge teeth in Lion's mouth she knew it would falter, leaving her tender flesh vulnerable. She thought about running, trying to find higher ground. Maybe seeking out the Tin Woodman, who had broached the idea of an alliance the night before.

But before she could act, Lion flew through the air, mighty jaws bared.

Dorothy held up her left arm for protection and Lion crunched his teeth down on it. The armor held but started collapsing around her elbow, and for a moment she was sure Lion would rip her arm, armor and all, free from her body. She tried to pull back but Lion held tight, thick bloodied saliva oozing onto her chin and chest.

"*Lion,*" she screamed and she squirmed sharply; she heard a small bone break but was able to pull her arm free of the leather strap that had protected it. She tumbled to the dirt below, Lion left with the armor in his huge mouth. It took several moments for him to shake it free, as he had penetrated the leather and it stuck to his canines.

Dorothy hit the ground hard and rolled. She sensed it was not just the strap around her arm that had been pulled free; lying in the dirt and blood she looked down to see the cuirass which had protected her chest had been ripped to tatters and hung by a strap, leaving her vulnerable from the navel up.

Lion lowered his huge head and took a mighty step forward. The low rumble from his throat made the earth shake beneath his feet.

Dorothy lay on her back propped up by her hands, her legs flat on the ground and her silver slippers hanging from her feet. She began to inch backward, and while she was one to have a cheery disposition there was nothing cheery in the giant figure looming over her, the thick blood drenched saliva dribbling down on her feet. She burst into terrified tears and just then the sound of Scarecrow screaming in pain could be heard, piercing.

Dorothy threw her hands over her ears and shook her head, weeping. They had all been friends, they had adventured together. It was one thing fighting the Wicked Witch of the West or the Nome King, but to die like this? Hearing the screams of one of her dearest friends as another ripped her to pieces? It was too horrible.

The tears flowed wildly and she whispered, *"No, no no no,"* over and over. The agonizing moment took so long that she realized she had not, in fact, been disemboweled. She opened her eyes and saw Lion looking down at her, his own eyes filling with tears.

"Oh Dorothy," he said, giant tears raining down on her. "I'm sorry Dorothy, I'm so sorry."

Dorothy threw her arms up and wrapped them around Lion's thick mane. She held him tight for a moment then pressed a button hidden in her right sleeve. A blade shot out, penetrating Lion's skull and planting itself in his brain. His body spasmed for a moment; piss and shit spilled down, some soiling Dorothy. Then the beast collapsed on top of her. Dorothy lay, breathing hard, assessing the damage.

"You always were a coward," Dorothy finally said, moving to wriggle out from beneath the giant beast.

In the background, Scarecrow screamed.

24 Hours Earlier

DOROTHY GALE PACED in the small, dusty room.

"This is all?" she demanded, frustrated. Scattered about herself, in various positions of relaxation, annoyance and tension, the few who had responded to her call had gathered. "Just the four of us?"

"Well if you wanted to get us together, why'd you ask us to meet in this *dump*?" the Tin Woodman said, lazily swinging his axe about, the same axe that had once chopped off all his own limbs (only to have them replaced with tin). "I mean, pretty stupid."

"Don't be mean to Dorothy," Scarecrow said, nervously picking at his own straw and then replacing it back within his overalls.

"Maybe you should have talked to the *best* thinker in Oz before deciding to meet here," the Tin Woodman groused, giving Scarecrow a nasty smirk.

Scarecrow did not rise to the bait; he knew he was one of the two best thinkers in all of Oz, and he was not about to start arguing the designation.

Dorothy looked at them, irritated. Maybe the Tin Woodman was right; this had been a mistake. She knew they needed to talk, had needed to since they had seen that brutal, violent footage 48 hours earlier. But after watching the horrible pictures they had all just returned to their homes, replicas of the world they had inhabited when they had lived in the real Oz. They all pretended what they had just seen would not be pushed on them, despite the express words spoken. That they would be *forced* to do the same thing.

Dorothy looked to Lion but he was clearly distracted; he knew how short their time was before they were to be put into battle, and he did not want to spend it here. He lay on the ground on his back, his four giant paws in the air, as if studying the length and sharpness of his claws. They were indeed long, and indeed sharp.

For just a moment Dorothy imagined what those claws would feel like slicing across her torso, but she quickly shook that thought away. Lion had saved her so many times (and she, him!) that the mere thought was too horrible to bear. She shook her head and let her eyes go around the room, the only one that clearly did not come from the land of Oz. It reminded her somewhat of a large room from her home in Kansas, but with a more exotic feel. The walls were of stone instead of wood; the furniture had a curvature emphasis rather than the rigid, straight tables and chairs she grow up around in Auntie Em's home.

The Tin Woodman's eyes followed Dorothy's and his narrowed. "Oh yes, *this* was a place to get all to gather. Not in the Land of the Winkies where I happen to be king and we would have met in splendor!"

"Why your home," growled Lion, not looking up, tapping the tips of his claws together. "In the Forest of the Wild Beasts we could stay under the splendor of the skies, where I rule!"

Scarecrow fingered his blue hat nervously. Since he had been awakened (not by the Powder of Life, as some thought) he had tried to show wisdom in his words. "My mansion is *in* the Winkie Country and Jack Pumpkinhead designed guest rooms for all my closest friends…"

"I would have thought the Wizard would be here," Dorothy said, to herself.

Scarecrow bristled but did not reply.

"Well *we* are," the Tin Woodman said. "So what is it you want to discuss, that you drag us to this shithole in what could be our last day drawing breath?"

Dorothy turned on him and exhaled sharply. "I wanted to discuss tomorrow!"

The Tin Woodman tried to hold her gaze but he turned away, unable. After he had chopped his own arms and legs off after that cunt of a Wicked Witch had enchanted his axe because he had committed the unthinkable of falling in love with someone he wasn't supposed to, his torso had been taken as well, all replaced with tin. He had tried to remain true to himself but eventually turned cold, and nasty, and in this manner he had stumbled upon Dorothy and Scarecrow for the first time. They had convinced him it was worth it to try to reclaim the old feelings he used to have. In reality, not having a heart made life easier. When you don't give a crap about anything, nothing can hurt.

He had felt that same coldness seep in when, 48 hours before, they had been forced to watch the giant screen in this very same room. If he was going to be forced to fight those around him to the death, what good was a heart? It would just get in the way.

But sometimes memories seeped in, and the way his friends made him feel was too hard to suppress.

He looked away, hearing the squeak of his tin. "What is there to discuss."

"*That* door," Dorothy replied, pointing. All of them took a moment to look at the bright yellow door. "This room and *that* door are the only things that did not come from our home in Oz! Whoever is forcing us to do this—those two horrible men, whoever they are, wherever they come from—their secret must be behind that door!"

Dorothy had a way of speaking that gave others hope, especially her friends, and as they looked to the bright yellow door they realized she was right; if they could just get to the other side they might be able to figure out why they were here and, most importantly, not be forced to fight each other, as they had seen others be forced to do. But the Tin Woodman again felt a surge of disdain, perhaps even more reinforced by the fact he had been made to feel even the smallest shreds of hope.

"We *tried* Dorothy, or did you forget?"

Dorothy opened her mouth to respond but reluctantly closed it. Indeed, after they had seen the bloodshed and heartbreak on the giant screen they had attacked the door with gusto. Lion, the Hungry Tiger, and Jack Pumpkinhead put their strength together and tried to push, then pull the great yellow door ajar. Glinda than used all the magic she could muster and it resisted it all. The Tin Woodman himself had taken his axe to the door, even boasting that there had never been a door he could not set aside…only to also be thwarted in his efforts to break through.

"What is different now?" he said, and he had to admit he was darkly enjoying the look of despair that spread across Dorothy's face.

When no one responded (other than a terse look from Scarecrow, which he ignored) the Tin Woodman answered his own question, "Oh I know! Nothing!"

"Oh I just can't bear it!" Dorothy cried out, turning away from them. She was not one to cry, or whine, but this all seemed overwhelming. She kept seeing the boy and the small bear, chatting and weeping together on the big screen. The boy had been crying when the bear had offered his bare bear torso, only to have it take numerous stabs to finally land a deadly blow. *Good bye…Christopher Robin…*the bear had said, before passing into a bloody death.

"Dorothy," Scarecrow said, walking to her. She was huddled in the corner, where an opening in the back of the mundane room led to the beautiful valleys of Oz. In the horizon was the Yellow Brick Road. They could walk that road and it would take them to the Emerald City—though while it looked the same it was much closer here than in the real Oz. Everything looked as it did in Oz, and was situated as it was in Oz. But it was all closer and instead of there being many inhabitants there were far fewer. It seemed like whoever had done this had plucked out Scarecrow and his friends (and a few others he did not consider friends) and dropped them in a miniature version of their home, to live as they pleased…until.

Until it was time for the culling.

Dorothy was looking out in the distance at the yellow bricks, remembering her first adventure, when she and her companions had walked that very road (except in the real Oz). There had been numerous times during that adventure she thought they would be stopped, even killed. There were the wolves the Witch had set on them, who the Tin Woodman had slaughtered with his axe. There were the crows, who the Scarecrow had killed, snapping their necks with his bare hands. And of course there was the giant spider in the forest, who Lion had to ravage and kill.

Dorothy spun about suddenly, causing Scarecrow to lose his footing and topple backwards. "Surely if we could overcome those obstacles we will be able to work our way through one silly door!" she proclaimed.

None knew what thoughts had gone through her head, but they knew that Dorothy was not one to quit. And although Scarecrow was deemed one of the two best thinkers in the land, it was often Dorothy who worked out solutions when problems arose.

Lion sat up and looked at her, expectantly. Scarecrow, once he regained his footing, looked at her expectantly. And even the Tin Woodman could think of nothing negative to say.

Dorothy moved to speak, but she was stopped by a sound from the other side of the room. From the yellow door.

They all turned and looked.

It was that same door, the one they had just been discussing. From the other side they heard bolts being tossed and locks being turned.

"What the," the Tin Woodman muttered, then he jumped back. They all jumped back.

For slowly, the door had begun to open.

48 Hours Earlier

AT FIRST DOROTHY HAD BEEN

PLEASED, but that soon turned to discomfort, and even

fear.

She had been pleased that her dear dear friend Scarecrow
had wanted to meet with her, and had the simply delicious idea
they walk the Yellow Brick Road but *away* from Emerald City.

He had asked her via a note, and as she had strolled
down the path she had thought of other adventures they had
enjoyed together. Her meandering thoughts were distracted
when she noted, up and down the path, others who she knew
(many she was fond of, some not so much) seemed to have the
same destination in mind. There were Lion and the Hungry
Tiger, giggling and strolling regally as if they were still pulling a
chariot of royalty. There was the Tin Woodman. And the
Wizard himself, balloons floating above his head, self-
importantly strolling down the path. But why was Glinda
there—and the Nome King, a true enemy of Oz? And the Witch
of the West, her pale, bloodless skin almost glowing under the
sun, her eye patch in place concealing the hole where her second
eye should be. Why would she be here?

Dorothy caught up to Jack Pumpkinhead, who greeted her pleasantly but then acknowledged that he didn't know why so many were walking this path, only that he himself had received a note from Glinda asking him to go. And Dorothy excused herself to hurry ahead, only to be told by the Wizard that he was walking the path because he had received a note requesting it—from Dorothy herself! As she could remember writing no such note, she grew more and more apprehensive.

The path ended at what seemed to be a fairly folksy home, but one that did not look like it belonged in Oz at all. They all stared at it, most with distaste, before entering.

Soon they were all crowded together in what appeared to be the only room within the house's walls. Dorothy's companions were ill impressed by the size and accommodations. Dorothy had tried to explain that where she came from there were many homes much like this, at least in size and shape. None seemed overly interested, and some made mention to leave when suddenly, the giant screen lowered from the ceiling.

"Why, whatever is *that*?" Scarecrow proclaimed. "As one of the two greatest thinkers in Oz, even I have never thought of a device such as that!"

The Wizard rolled his eyes but said nothing.

The presence of the screen quieted the talk of leaving, and they even found chairs (some plopping on the floor comfortably) and faced it.

"Why, I have no idea," Dorothy said.

"I heard of such things before coming to live in Oz," the Wizard said, stroking his chin, throwing a smug look toward Scarecrow. " I believe it is for displaying moving pictures."

"A form of magic then," Glinda said, pushing her long red hair back. "As long as it holds no threat to us, I will allow it."

Just then the lights in the room started to darken, and even as a bit of panic surged through them it was quelled once a picture formed on the screen.

At first Dorothy was thrilled—and she sensed all around her, her companions were all equally excited. On the screen she saw a table, sitting in a beautiful field. Why, it almost looked like Oz it was so lovely! And then animals appeared, and she knew the screen was indeed showing her a world as magical as Oz as the animals were chatting away as old friends.

The room full of magical and mystical creatures grew silent in awe of the action on the screen.

"Look at the bear!" the Hungry Tiger suddenly shouted out, and all laughed appreciatively. For the bear was indeed small and sweet and strolled about like a large munchkin, with his round stomach pushed out.

"Naked, though!" Lion added. He always made sure to at least have a bow in his mighty mane.

"Quiet, I think they are speaking!" Wizard shouted, which was needed as excited chatter started filling the room.

From the screen the bear *was* speaking.

"Could you pass the honey, Piglet?" the bear said. "Oh would you, could you, pass some delicious honey, my honey?"

The small pig reached out at far as he could, but his arms weren't long enough to get the bottle across the table. "I'm trying Winnie, but my arms are too short," he said, his voice a small squeak. "Too short too short, they are ever too short!"

"A pig with arms, how *adorable!*" Dorothy proclaimed.

The Hungry Tiger sat up in attention. "Is there a tiger? There should be a tiger!"

"There is no tiger," Lion said with a chuckle, which caused the Hungry Tiger to snort in indignation.

To add to the cuteness a small kangaroo appeared on the table and, hopping across it, carried the honey to the bear.

"Good job Roo!" a larger kangaroo said, as Roo hopped back to her.

"That's a good little Roo there, Kanga," a donkey at the end of the table said, his voice weighed down and heavy. "A good, good Roo."

"Thank you Eeyore," said Kanga, tapping Roo on the head.

It was indeed quite a quaint scene, and Dorothy and her companions were enjoying the moving pictures very much.

Suddenly, however, the video became blurry, so much so that none could make out what was happening at the picnic table. Worse, when the footage again became clear it was no longer showing the adorable group of animals in the scenic park, but rather it was focusing on two figures, who seemed to be staring directly at them.

One of the people was a man, who had a face so gaunt it looked like flesh on a skeleton. A puff of white hair rested on his head and he had a long, narrow nose. He also had a small smirk, as if greatly amused by what he was seeing.

The other wore a mask over his face so that none of his features were visible. There were horrible black and white streaks across it, like a madman's chess board. Two black circles were drawn onto the mask where the eyes should have been

"They're hideous!" Dorothy cried out.

"Where did the cute animals go?" Scarecrow asked.

Even the Witch of the West, unliked by all and with little interest in acquiring popularity, peered her one eye away, not wanting to look at the two figures that had appeared in front of them.

The unmasked man spoke. His voice was low and dark.

"The culling of the 100 Acre Wood has begun."

In the strange room, like a room in Kansas but not really, the residents of Oz stared.

The pictures before them once again blurred, and when they came into focus they were back at the picnic table within, presumably, the 100 Acre Wood.

At first Dorothy felt relief; surely the cute animals were better viewing than those two horrible figures! But the relief soon turned to horror as she realized what she was seeing.

The table which had held the picnic had been overturned. Food and drink had been tossed everywhere, and the adorable talking pig who walked on two legs and whose arms weren't long enough to pass the honey was sprawled against the table in a red puddle.

"Is that…jam about Piglet?" Dorothy asked, feeling dazed.

Then the bear, his coat clearly smeared red, approached Piglet, bent down and picked him up in his jaws.

"It's not jam," the Hungry Tiger said breathlessly, and it added to no one's mood that his stomach noticeably rumbled loudly. A pig may not be a baby, but he suspected it would be quite delicious.

Winnie bit down and a small squeak escaped as the last of life was chewed out of Piglet. Winnie flung his mouth back and forth ferociously, the small pig twisted to and fro, before Winnie opened his jaws and threw Piglet's lifeless body across the field.

Winnie turned on Roo, who was trying to hop toward his mother. Roo had been injured in the melee, and was struggling.

"Get back here you hopper you clopper you sopper, get back here you little bastard," Winnie the chubby little bear said, and he lunged toward the small kangaroo.

Kanga leaped forward and caught Winnie with a kick across the side of his head, sending him sprawling. "Hop Roo, hop!" Kanga cried, but clearly Roo was more injured than was first thought. He took another hop then fell over. He tried to crawl toward his mother.

"Help me!" he cried. "Help, Momma!"

The wind had been knocked from Winnie for a moment, but he was back on his feet, snarling. He started to charge at Kanga, his teeth and claws prepared for battle.

"Dear Lord," Dorothy said, unable to breathe, unable to look away.

Kanga leapt in front of Winnie but lost her footing; teeth first Winnie bit into Kanga's chest. Kanga collapsed back, but lying on her back was able to get one kick off, again sending Winnie sprawling. She tried to get up but soon realized she had been wounded too severely and was quickly bleeding out.

"Momma!" Roo said, stumbling to her side. "*Momma!*"

Kanga's dry tongue lapped Roo across his forehead. "It's…it's okay," she whispered.

Winnie was struggling back to his feet. He leveled his ferocious gaze on the injured kangaroos.

"We need to go," Roo said, pulling at his mother's ears. "Please, we need to go."

"We will go, we will be safe," Kanga said, though some words were gargled with the blood filling her chest. "Come…closer…"

Roo leaned in and with the last of her strength Kanga snapped the smaller kangaroo's neck. Roo was motionless in her arms, before folding down on himself.

"*Noooo*," Kanga gargled as Winnie landed on her chest, shredding muscle down to the heart.

"Stop this, stop this!" Dorothy said, finally standing.

"We're locked...we're locked in!" It was Scarecrow who had gone to the door by which they had entered.

Several others, including the Tin Woodman and Lion, went and banged on the doors and windows to take them back to the Yellow Brick Road, to the replica of Oz. But the doors and windows would not budge.

They all slowly returned to their spots within the small room. Lion was closing his eyes and the Hungry Tiger held him tight. The Wizard was shaking his giant head, the balloons above him bouncing about, and Glinda had taken to plotting how they could all escape this horrible place. Even the Nome King and Witch of the West had seen enough, and they both cheerfully lived in squalor and pain.

The picnic was now soaked in blood. Winnie had been feasting, but he seemed to become aware of what he had done, and sat in the middle of the mayhem and cried loudly. He even went to the different creatures that he had mauled and held them, kissed them. He carried Roo's body around like a doll, explaining that all would be all right, that this was all some kind of dream, like the time he dreamed he had found bees that did not make honey. *No honey, no honey, so sad with no honey* he repeated over and over again.

Another figure, dazed but at the moment unhurt, stumbled into the clearing.

It was a little boy, wearing a red hat.

"Why Christopher Robin!" said Winnie, still clutching Roo's dead body tight. "Look at what has happened! So bad, so sad, my dear friend Christopher Robin!"

Christopher looked at the dead animals everywhere, tears running down his face. "It's like Mr. Teller said," he finally gasped. "I didn't believe."

"It is so horrible," Winnie replied. He looked at his own bloody fur, tried to wipe away some of it, just smeared it deeper and sat down in a puddle of kangaroo blood, despondent.

"*What have I done*," he moaned, still holding the dead baby kangaroo. "*No fun, good done, what oh what oh what have I done.*"

"Finish it," Christopher Robin said simply. "Please. End this for me, now. Please."

"No, no, no no," Winnie replied.

Christopher Robin sat down so heavily a puddle of blood sprinkled up as high as his chin. He did not bother to wipe it away.

"You know the first rule, the drool, the rule: we cannot end our own life so please, let it be you just you," Christopher Robin said. "I do not want it to be me, not me, you see, not me."

Winnie himself was wallowing in blood (the only difference being he had spilled much of it). The blood lust he had succumbed to seemed to have passed and he was not motivated to finish what he had started. The bodies of his friends scattered all around him drained any desire to kill Christopher Robin.

"They will kill us both if we just sit here, they will, they kill," moaned Winnie.

Christopher Robin took his red hat off and stared at it; a piece of normalcy in a world that had been upended.

Winnie stood up suddenly, determined. He walked to the overturned picnic table, ignoring all the gore. He fell to his hands and knees and eventually found it under Owl's body; a sharp knife which had been laid out for the picnic. His hands were still small nubs but his protracted claws were sharp and nimble. He picked up the knife and carried it to Christopher Robin.

"Please oh please, hold this, Christopher Robin."

Christopher Robin's eyes opened wide and he shook his head violently.

"Oh please oh jeez," Winnie said, and he picked up Christopher Robin's hand and placed the knife in it.

The boy looked at his oldest truest friend and just shook his head, tears running down his face.

Winnie touched Christopher Robin's cheek with a gentle but blood stained paw. "I will take care of all, you neither have to cut nor maul."

Then Winnie carefully maneuvered Christopher Robin's hand so the knife was facing straight up. Then he leapt in the air and landed across the blade, feeling it rip into his chest. It did not quite penetrate deep enough, and Winnie cried out in pain. In the end Christopher Robin had to stab Winnie several times, until finally a thick stream of blood bubbled out of his mouth and the dying bear fell to the ground. Christopher Robin screamed and stepped back as the blood soaked him, he losing his grip on the knife. Winnie lay, the knife further driven up through his rib cage and tearing his heart to pieces. He turned on his back, gasping for air, blood spraying from his mouth.

"*Winnie*," Christopher Robin screamed.

"Good...bye...Christopher...Rob...in" Winnie lost the last word in swallowed blood.

Christopher Robin hugged the bear, weeping. He finally pushed himself to his feet, blood smeared all over his clothes and body. He looked about himself at the dead bodies of all his friends, then he started to scream.

"*I'm the last one, what more do you want?*" He spun about, looking to the sky. "*You said there had to be one left, so take me, take me now, I don't care how TAKE ME NOW*"

Dorothy did not even know tears were running down her face till they sprinkled down on her lap. All the animals were dead and only one was left…what was to happen next?

She was going to speak; all the creatures of Oz stared in horrified muteness. Before she could say anything they all heard another sound from the screen.

It was the sound of footsteps. An animal moving quickly.

Christopher Robin spun about, confused, when Eeyore the donkey barreled toward him. Eeyore leapt in the air, his front hooves landing squarely on Christopher Robin's skull and driving it into the ground. The boy's arms flailed for a moment, then his head exploded like a piece of rotted fruit under the donkey's weight. Eeyore bucked up and down using his hooves to drive Christopher Robin's brains and skull into the bloody dirt.

After a time he stopped, breathing hard. Then he cried out, "Happy happy, not sappy or crappy, Eeyore finally feels so very happy!"

Dorothy felt a bile fill her throat and thought she might vomit; around her others were also gagging, and Jack Pumpkinhead had retreated to the doors and windows which took them back to the Yellow Brick Road and was banging on them.

Just then the picture on the screen went black.

Dorothy looked around herself, hoping for some reassurance from the figures about her. Each of her friends (and her not so much friends) stared slack jawed at the screen, still trying to process what they had seen. Even the Tin Woodman, who never showed fear, clutched his axe to his chest with hands that were clearly shaking. Even the Witch of the West's bloodless white skin seemed even paler.

The screen burst back into life in front of them, eliciting gasps. It focused on the two horrible figures again, one with the black and white checkered mask, the other with no mask but a cold, sneering veneer that offered no warmth. For Dorothy they were better than the blood stained wreck of the 100 Acre Wood, but the men still filled her with an ominous horror, a feeling of helplessness and loss.

The unmasked man gave the smallest of smiles—even chuckling, in a hideous way!—and then spoke.

"The culling is successfully complete," the Unmasked Man said. "Eeyore the Donkey is victorious and is the Champion of the 100 Acre Wood. He will move to the Champion round. We can agree it was riveting and an appropriate end for beasts and child alike. Would you not agree?"

Dorothy did not know to whom the question was addressed, but she found herself shaking her head vigorously.

The Masked Man did not reply, neither with word nor gesture.

"I am glad you agree, Mr. Story," the Unmasked Man said. "In the end the Champions will meet for one final battle.

"The next battle will take place in three days' time: the culling of Oz. All inhabitants of the land of Oz will battle to the death. There will be one Champion."

Dorothy felt like she had been ripped from the ground, like she was spinning, like she would vomit. She opened her mouth and tried to catch her breath but could not. All around her the room was silent.

The Unmasked Man seemed to look right at her, but all in the room thought he had turned his dark gray eyes on them and was looking right into their souls.

"In three days' time," he said again, and the screen blinked black. Then slowly it raised, retracting into the ceiling.

The room remained dim, and slowly the lights raised.

The Hungry Tiger had been holding Lion tight, but as no one moved or spoke Lion, trembling, pulled free. He was noticeably shaking, and a puddle of pee was forming under him.

"Dear," Tiger said, alarmed. He had not seen Lion like this in, well, since his famous walk down the Yellow Brick Road when so many of their adventures began.

"*I have to get out of here*," Lion yelled, and he ran toward a yellow door that had been partially blocked by the screens. Lion threw himself at the door, snarling and clawing and growling.

"He's right!" the Wizard said from the back. "The door in the back will take us back to Oz, but that yellow door might lead to freedom!"

The Wizard was considered the best thinker in Oz, so suddenly the Lion's attack seemed less pathetic and more productive. The Hungry Tiger joined Lion and they started throwing their huge bodies against the door. There was no knob or device to turn to try to open it, but they scratched at the side of the door, trying to rip it free from the wall. Jack Pumpkinhead, who was tall and thin but strong, joined and they all pounded at the door.

"Step aside, Beasts," said the Tin Woodman, and as they parted, breathing hard, he readied his axe. "I've yet to meet a door that could stop me!"

Dorothy felt a surge of hope; she had seen the Tin Woodman do extraordinary things with that axe, and there was little doubt a door would succumb to its power!

But the first blow released a jarring sound and the axe flew from his hands, landing at the feet of Lion, who offered a small growl and leapt away.

"Just rusty I guess," the Tin Woodman said, picking the axe up again. But after several more chops it became clear his tin arms were the only thing weakening, and the yellow door was as solid and unyielding as when he began.

"Let magic show the way!" cried Glinda, moving to the front of the room. From a small pouch at her side she pulled several ingredients and when she threw them to the ground at the foot of the door thick smoke began to rise.

All the others offered an *ooooh* and Dorothy felt a rise of hope…but when the smoke cleared the door remained, as solid as before.

Glinda might be known as Glinda the Good but that did not mean she did not have a pragmatic side, which rose to the surface when she felt herself or others threatened. She concentrated and attempted to do a most delicate of magic, to bring the inanimate door to life (as had been done with Jack Pumpkinhead, who had retreated to the back of the room). It had a risky element as giving any object free will leaves up to chance what that object will do with that will; Glinda felt confident she could make the door understand that letting them out was certainly preferable to being hacked and burned to death.

But like the attacks of claw and girth, axe and strength, the magic resulted in no change. The solid yellow door remained in front of them, as solid (and as yellow) as ever. More solid, Dorothy thought, if that made sense (to Dorothy it did).

"Get out of my way," the Wicked Witch of the West said, and with one leap stood before the door, an ominous presence despite her small stature, missing eye and six misshapen pony tails that had green straggly hair going in all directions at once.

All usually stood clear of her, and all certainly felt comfortable dodging out of her way now. She waved her hands in front of the door for a moment, then looked to the back of the room, where locked door and windows kept them from returning to Oz.

"You might want to…move," she said, offering a small chuckle. Just then the windows and doors back to Oz burst open and Winged Monkeys and wolves poured into the room.

"That's it, that's it," the Witch cried, as the animals swarmed the yellow door, banging and biting and clawing. *"Get that door open, and free us from this place once and for all."*

One of the monkeys looked at her and she waved a cap at it, *"I own you till your debt is repaid, I still have your cap. Now tear that door down!"*

The monkey squeaked then joined his brethren. Soon, though, the monkeys and wolves (and even bees, buzzing about the edges of the door) were collapsed in exhaustion in front of the door, with no progress having been made.

The Witch's action did have a different result, as now there was nothing keeping the inhabitants of the small dingy room from returning to the replica of Oz that had been created for them. One by one, starting with Jack Pumpkinhead and Glinda (who was embarrassed by her failure, her face as red as her hair), they all filed out of the room, back to their makeshift homes, despite now carrying the knowledge that in three days' time they would be expected to take part in some kind of battle to the death, much as they had just witnessed.

"Wait!" Dorothy called, as the exhausted wolves and monkeys followed the Wicked Witch of the West out. The Hungry Tiger and Lion spared her a sympathetic glance but they too could spend no more time in this horrible little room having horrible little thoughts.

"Please, wait!" she cried again, but none would heed her call. Even her nearest and dearest had had enough of this room for the moment, and soon Dorothy was alone.

She was not one to cry, or sing sad longing songs, or wallow in difficulties. She clicked her silver shoes together (the bottom was a bit green, perhaps due to copper in the stream in which Dorothy bathed and washed her belongings) and cried out, *"I will get this door open, I will figure this out, even if I must go at it alone!"*

***

DOROTHY SPENT THE NEXT DAY

wandering the land of Oz, trying to rally support and camaraderie to prepare to put up a fight against the horrible figures they had seen on the screen.

She had little luck, and the more she travelled the more she became aware of how limited this version of Oz truly was from the one she remembered.

In the land of the Winkies she heard little sound nearby, and certainly not the constant drum beat of the yellow creatures.

During her many years in Oz she had matured and found close friendships with the Winkies. But now in this new Oz, she had found a pleasure she had not known before with them. Winkies, who were very good at construction, were able to make many toys that fit her unique tastes.

She had sought out the Tin Woodman, who long before had been made ruler of the land. She would not have minded spending some time with the many partners she'd had who resided here. There was Blinkie and Twinkie, and particularly Dinkie, with whom she had shared bed and intimate metal works since arriving at the new Oz.

None were here now, and while in the distance she could see Winkies dancing and frolicking, when she attempted to grow close they seemed to fade away, never being within an auditory call. It struck her that there was some kind of new magic afoot, in which there was the appearance that Winkies were around when in reality there were none, all their fun and satisfying toys gone too. Just like it appeared they all were still residing in the Land of Oz when they really were in this fake shrunken land that felt like Oz and looked like Oz but was in fact not Oz.

The Tin Woodman would not answer her call; she followed up this failure seeking out Scarecrow. He too was not available, as he had locked himself in his home and he was thinking as hard as he could. He was one of the two best thinkers in the land (as he told all who would listen, and even those who did not) and he thought that if he just thought on what he needed to think about it, all would be illuminated. At least, that's what he thought.

She then went to the Forest of Enormous Beasts and waded through the trees looking for her dearest and bravest of friends. She hesitated when she heard the gratification of Lion and the Hungry Tiger. For a short time the sounds aroused her, but then she became a bit disgusted by some of the inner thoughts between the two they shared during the intimacy, thoughts turned to words that were meant for the two of them and no others. Some of them were just…gross.

In the end Dorothy spoke to none of them, but she did make sure to leave notes to all, requesting they meet with her back in the 'strange foreign cabin' to discuss their options, and how they would evade suffering a similar fate of the poor inhabitants of the 100 Acre Wood. She had a little bit of a giggle when after she left the note for Lion and Hungry Tiger she had stepped into a clearing out of their sight when she heard them find the note. Lion read it aloud, then Dorothy heard as Tiger said *she wasn't just here, was she*, and Lion responded *no way she could have heard me call you my big juicy bear bear, right?*

She continued to spread her message, to Jack Pumpkinhead, and Glinda, and the Nome King. Surprisingly, the only one who bothered to talk to her was the Wicked Witch of the West.

She lived in a castle that towered high in the sky at the western most point of the Oz replica. Dorothy had made it to the bottom and began chugging her way to the top. One step after another, she was exhausted! It was a good thing she was an athletic marvel, spending so much of her time with the Winkies and the unique work outs they offered, as well as the constant wrestling tournaments she took part in.

She made it to the top floor, where the Wicked Witch was clearly waiting for her. Dorothy hadn't passed a single door or room on the way up, nor was there a bench or chair for her to rest for even a moment. She even noticed that when she stopped walking for the mildest of breathers the tower seemed to move further away, so the only way to get there was to walk directly without so much as a moment's rest.

The staircase ended in a big beautiful room, and the Witch was sprawled out on a couch like throne, smoking a strange smelling substance from a large glass pipe. As Dorothy entered the room the Witch lit up the edge of her finger and placed it in a bowl filled with the green shake; it burned bright orange and the pipe filled with thick white smoke. It soon disappeared into the Witch's lungs. She held it there for a moment, then pointed to a glass on the table.

"I tried to poison it, but it didn't take, so drink," she said, exhaling thick smoke.

Dorothy was parched from the walk but she had a history with this Witch, and she approached the glass tentatively, before just shaking her head.

The Wicked Witch had no time for nonsense. "Drink it you foolish little twat and tell me what you're here to say."

Dorothy only hesitated a second. She had so many memories of the Wicked Witch trying to cause harm—and even death!—to her, but now she just sat on her couch holding her hookah with a slightly glazed look in her green eyes.

She picked up the glass and brought it to her lips…and it was empty.

"Why, there's nothing here to drink at all!" she exclaimed, her throat parched.

"You think I would give you water, you silly little twat?" the Wicked Witch laughed. "If I can't poison you at least I could fuck with you." She laughed again, then shook her head. "Give Dorothy water. My goodness, you could throw it in my face and melt me right here! No, I didn't work hard to poison you, and accept that as a gift to your dry throat!"

Dorothy was unsure how to respond but the Witch stared at her with her solid green eyes so she finally said, "Thank you?"

The Witch chortled at that. "'Thank you', she says. Ah, gratitude. If I had my way I would have poisoned you, leaving eggs within you that would birth roaches that would feast from the inside out. That would leave you sneezing and shitting blood till you finally choked on your own thickened phlegm. But thank you, you say? You're quite welcome. So please, tell me why you're harassing me so you can go on your way. If I can't kill you today I very much want to see you walking away."

"Stop being so mean!" Dorothy cried out. "We must have a meeting to come up with a plan for what we will do when they try to force us to take part in their miserable game of killing!"

"'Force me'? Dorothy, you are dumber than you look, dumber than that tiger fucking friend of yours, dumber than Glinda, who, by the way, is just angered I wouldn't go along with her 'experimentation' phase when she was in college.

"No one is forcing me to do anything. I will gladly take part in the game, and will happily send my creatures upon you with great vengeance and furious anger and laugh as they pull you to pieces."

Dorothy was a bit overwhelmed with the lack of empathy she was receiving, but she would not let the Witch see this. "Mean!" she cried out.

"Of course it might all be for naught," the Witch mused, in-between inhaling and exhaling another great pillar of white smoke. "If that creature of yours has grown bigger, and even more dangerous. I have not seen the bastard, but we think he is here?"

Dorothy grew quiet at that. "Under the ground," she said softly.

"Ah! Yes! I saw the trees shaking about the time he usually takes his shits and scratches away the dirt nearby. Won't that be interesting, if he comes up to play?"

"I am trying to save everyone!" Dorothy cried out.

The Witch sighed, resigned. "If I send out your message to the other creatures of Oz, will you leave me the fuck alone?" she asked.

Dorothy was taken aback. "I, uh, yes! If you tell them to meet in the strange room we met when we watched the other animals fight to the death! Tomorrow, when the sun and moon change places!"

The Witch snapped her fingers. Several Winged Monkeys appeared in the room. They kept their distance from the Witch, uncomfortably shifting from one foot to the other.

"*I still have the hat so get your shit smelling asses over here!*" the Witch cackled.

"Of course, Master," the largest of the monkeys said.

"You were eavesdropping Franky, hoping this little twat would kill me so you would be freed?"

The monkey nodded his head. "Of course."

"Not yet, turd eater. Now go, spread the word. Little Dorothy the twat wants to meet everyone tomorrow at dusk. In the shit hole."

"Of course, Master."

"*Of course, Master,*" the Witch mocked. "Get out, get out!"

The monkeys took flight and were soon gone from the tower.

Dorothy was still stunned. "T-thank you," she said again.

"Oh, more gratitude! I will tell you what. You can thank me when I rip your head from your body and shit down your neck once the culling of Oz begins!"

"We will meet and come up with a plan to save Oz!" Dorothy said defiantly.

The Witch shrugged at that. "Nobody will come," she said.

Dorothy reddened. She walked toward the top of the staircase, but turned sharply. "I have fought you before, Witch, and I always come out victorious! On land, on the sea, in the clouds. Wherever we fight, it is always I who wins!"

The Witch smiled at that. "This isn't that kind of story, twat."

***

THE WITCH'S WORDS RANG IN DOROTHY'S EARS, especially when the only few who gathered at her request at the mangy un-Oz like room were Lion, who seemed stressed, Scarecrow, who seemed distracted and deep in thought, and the Tin Woodman, who was hostile and snapped at everything and anything she said. Not even the Wizard had bothered to show.

Dorothy had suggested they needed to break through the yellow door, the one that separated them from the world of their captors. In an ever so cheerful manner the Tin Woodman had coldly pointed out that they had all been together the last time, and they had all given it a go to smash that door open, and it had resisted all attempts.

We must try, we must keep trying, we must ALWAYS keep trying was what Dorothy was preparing to say…when they heard a sound from that very same door. After hearing bolts pulled and locks thrown, the yellow door slowly began to open toward them.

"It's…it's opening!" Lion blurted out, and now they all stood in the small room, watching in sheer amazement. Indeed, the door that seemed to separate them from their captors (from freedom, perhaps?) was slowly pushing open toward them. Dorothy stood first, with the Tin Woodman clutching his axe behind her, and Scarecrow behind him, and finally Lion, taking his place in the rear.

They hovered like that for a moment, watching as the door slowly opened wide…and then *they* walked in.

Dorothy gasped. Since she had been in Oz she had witnessed extraordinary beings. Witches and Wizards and Kings and Queens. But for the first time in her life she could not quite catch her breath as she realized she might indeed be in the presence of *gods*.

"Yes, yes, we are here," the man said, as he entered. There were two of them, one with a masked face covered in checkerboard marks and two black dots for eyes and one thoroughly unmasked, with a long thin nose and eyes that stared with little compassion.

"H-Hello," Dorothy managed to squeak out. The same horrible people from the screen! Who had orchestrated all those adorable and sweet characters…beating and biting each other to death.

"I guess we should introduce ourselves," the man said. "I am Mr. Teller. This, is Mr. Story."

Mr. Story, who did not seem to speak under the wrapping, offered the smallest of bows.

Mr. Teller eyed the four characters, a look of annoyance and amusement on his face. "And I would think you should be preparing for tomorrow. What, may I ask, are you all doing here?"

Scarecrow stepped forward. He took a hat from his head and held it in front of his chest. "Well, uh, that's what we wanted to discuss with you, uh, perhaps," he said. Scarecrow had a way of speaking which suggested he was still the bumpkin he felt himself to be when life was granted to him in the field so many years before (and it was not brought to him by the Powder of Life, which had brought Jack Pumpkinhead to life, but rather from an enchanted goblet, brought to him by a man in armor who called himself King Arthur. King Arthur had been amazed at how the magical goblet had brought life where there had been none, and was to take part in other experiments with other creatures, animate and inanimate throughout Oz, when Glinda arrived, not too pleased with his presence. An immediate fight broke out which only concluded…oh, another story for another time. Another story, another time). But beneath Scarecrow's humbling mannerisms his eyes were taking in all.

"We were wondering how we wound up from *our* Oz to *this* Oz," he concluded, still clutching the hat to his straw chest.

"Well, don't you like this version of Oz?" Mr. Teller asked, as if surprised by the question.

The Tin Woodman had little of the patience or willingness to debase himself that Scarecrow displayed, and he stepped forward, holding his axe in a threatening manner.

"I'm guessing you didn't hear the question because you have too much blubber in your ears," he said, as the others jumped away from his threatening axe. "He asked you how we wound up *here*, and wants to know when we can go *back*."

Dorothy and Lion stepped aside quickly, almost pinned against the far wall. Scarecrow sighed and just stepped back.

"Oh, you're asking us, are you?" Mr. Teller said, and he reached up and snapped his fingers.

In an instant a parchment appeared in Mr. Story's left hand, and in his right hand was a quill with black ink dripping from the end.

"'Nick Chopper, aka the Tin Woodman, angrily stood before the gods. He thought he was in control of the situation but suddenly found that the arm that clutched the axe did not feel like his own'." Mr. Teller spoke as if reciting a tale, and as he spoke Mr. Story's pen hit the parchment at a ridiculous speed.

"Hey," the Tin Woodman said, looking at his arm. "What's happening here?"

Mr. Teller continued. "'He turned to the side of the room, where his friend Dorothy cowered against the wall'."

The Tin Woodman felt his body turn. His eyes widened in shock and horror. "No! No!" he called out.

"Please, stop!" Dorothy cried.

Mr. Teller did not stop. He spoke, and with every word uttered Mr. Story's pen hit the parchment. "'He pulled his arm back and flung the axe through the air, directly at Dorothy's head'."

"*No!*" Dorothy cried.

"Get out of the Ozma damn way, Dorothy!" the Tin Woodman said, his body still not his own. He threw the axe straight and with great purpose.

"'The throw was true, but at the last moment the axe soared higher, just removing some hair from the top of Dorothy's head'."

And like that, the axe smashed inches from Dorothy's forehead, pinning her to the wall by her long brown hair. She yanked, and some of her hair pulled free as she staggered away from the wall.

"Enough foolishness?" Mr. Teller asked, his dancing eyes leveled on the Tin Woodman.

A low growl filled the room and all turned to Lion, who was down on four legs, a fancy blue bow in his mane trembling from the vibrations emanating from his mighty throat.

"He had an axe to throw," Lion said stepping forward, his huge teeth bared. "And it has been thrown."

Mr. Teller sighed. He did not snap his fingers this time, merely said, "'The Hungry Tiger stepped out of his cave and was surprised to find his paw sinking in the sand. For surely they would have realized there was sinking sand outside their fuck den, yes? At first he was not alarmed, but when he tried to pull out he found he could not. The sinky sand was the sinkiest sand he had ever encountered, and he quickly started to disappear within'."

"What?" Lion said, confused. He looked over his shoulder but surely could not see all the way to his Forest home from this room.

"'The Hungry Tiger tried desperately to get his footing'," Mr. Teller continued, all the while Mr. Story's pen dotting across the parchment as fast as a humming bird darting from flower to flower. "'But alas, every time he put his paw down in hopes it would find solid ground it just sunk deeper. Soon the sinky sand was up to his chest. Then his neck. He realized there was no way he could get loose on his own, and he needed help. With all his strength he let out a mighty roar, one which could be heard throughout the kingdom—'"

A distant roar could be heard from across the land.

"'—but no one was close enough to get to his side before he would be swallowed up by the sinky sand. His mouth started to fill with the sand...'"

"Stop," Lion said, horror filling his heart.

"'And he let loose one final, muffled roar...'"

Another roar was heard, this time muted by the sand filling Tiger's throat, stomach, lungs.

"*Stop I beg of you,*" Lion said.

Mr. Teller did hesitate, and looked at Lion expectantly.

Lion frantically looked about himself as if there was an answer he could find. In the end all he could do was lie to the ground and roll over, his vulnerable underside fully visible.

"Please," he moaned.

Mr. Teller only hesitated one more instant before resuming. "'And then, at the last instant, the Hungry Tiger's paw hit hard ground. He pushed himself forward and found that the sand was not as deep, or as sinky, as it had first appeared. He wriggled his mighty hindquarters and was able to get first one, then two front paws to the solid ground outside the sand. Soon he had pulled himself totally out, stunned by how close to death he had just come. Even more surprisingly, when he reached back the sinky sand was gone, sunk back to the world below, replaced by hard soil above'."

They all stood in silence for a moment, and Mr. Teller finally nodded his head, satisfied. The parchment was immediately wrapped and disappeared within the jacket Mr. Story wore.

"All of you, are you ready to behave?" Mr. Teller stared at them.

There were several small head nods, and muttered sounds, but Mr. Teller was not satisfied. He looked to Mr. Story, whose face showed no expression behind the striped mask.

"No no, that will not do," Mr. Teller mused. "Perhaps another lesson?"

"No!" Lion exclaimed. Then, from the ground, he said, "We are…ready to behave."

"Everyone else?" Mr. Teller asked.

All of them, one after the other, offered the same promise.

"Good then," Mr. Teller replied. "Now that we got that unpleasantness out of the way. Why are you not back in your lands, enjoying yourselves? Preparing for battle?"

All were mute, unsure what they could say. Lion and the Tin Woodman still felt emasculated and just stared at the ground before them, Lion not even rolling back onto his front quarters. Scarecrow had placed his hat back on his head, but it was not helping with his thinking.

Dorothy stepped forward, pushing her hair back to cover her new bald spot. She was going to offer an explanation of how much this room reminded her of her beloved home in Kansas, but Mr. Teller held up a hand and silenced her with a gesture.

"It always happens," he said. "Before the culling. Those who believe they can outsmart the rules. I will tell you now, no one can outsmart us. Usually there is even one the day of, who thinks here is a loophole they have found. Do not go through that loophole, it will be worse for you, worse for all. So I suggest all go back to their homes, prepare, enjoy. For after all, is this world not better than the one you left?"

"With all due respect," Dorothy began, but she was cut off.

"Lion, when you lived in Oz, in *your* Oz, you had grown close to Tiger, is that not true?"

Lion, who was still demoralized and frustrated, muttered, "Of course."

"But you did not feel physical pleasure there, did you? That only started when you arrived here?"

Lion felt ridiculous lying on his back, his penis exposed during this whole exchange, so he rolled forward so his privates and vulnerables were pinned to the ground. "We began that...pleasure when we arrived here."

"Of course you did! The violence and sex here is so much realer, is it not? Dorothy, you didn't start exploring the Winkies as partners till you got here, is that not true?"

"Ewww, really Dorothy?" the Tin Woodman asked.

"Oh do shut up!" Dorothy replied, red.

"You don't get that in *your* Oz. Imagine if you had always been in *our* Oz?" Mr. Teller looked at her, and waited till, still flushed, she looked back.

"Oh, maybe," she replied.

"And the language you use. Was it nearly so…colorful when you were in your Oz?"

"Fuck no!" the Tin Woodman said.

"So go and enjoy! And tomorrow perhaps when the battle starts…perhaps you will enjoy that, as well?"

The four were still.

This did not bother Mr. Teller in the least. He offered a large smile. "And remember, one of you might get a happily ever after!"

Mr. Story nodded at this, then slowly turned his covered face and black dot eyes to each of them, giving each an equal and substantial case of the creeps. Then the two of them turned and took their exit.

Dorothy listened as the sound of locks and bolts were thrown on the other side of the yellow door, then footsteps echoing away.

"Why you, you, you," she said, her face red but with anger now, not embarrassment. "You will be the ones who will never get a happily ever after, you horrible people!" She stepped forward, breathing hard. She raised a fist defiantly at the door. "And you think we will enjoy hurting our friends? No, we will enjoy defeating you, you, you, you *witchfucker*."

"Yes, very brave and strong my dear girl. It might have more *oomph* to it if you had said it to them and not to a closed yellow door."

All turned to watch as the Wonderful Wizard of Oz waddled into the room.

"*Now* you show up?" the Tin Woodman said, walking across the room where his axe was still embedded into the wall. He gave it a yank, then a second, then a third when it pulled free. He blew the strands of Dorothy's hair off the blade then looked back to the tiny Wizard. "Perhaps you could have done us a lick of good if you'd been here when the goons were here!"

"Oh I guess I wasn't doing anything productive," the Wizard said in his coy way, gingerly moving forward, the multicolored balloons hovering over his head.

The Wizard had always been a small man, one of the smallest at the farm he grew up on in Omaha, Nebraska. But the longer he stayed in Oz the smaller he got, as he shrunk a little more every day. Soon he wasn't much bigger than a munchkin, making it to Dorothy's waist.

However, his studies made him the most learned thinker in all of Oz, and his brain continued to grow bigger and bigger. Naturally his skull had to expand to house such a magnificent brain, and soon his head was far far too heavy to be held up by his thin neck and weak body.

This indeed caused a conundrum, but one he solved looking back to his Omaha days. He found a surplus of helium festering under the ground and captured it in a tank. He now strapped this tank to his back and it had a tube that was attached to several balloons that soared over his head. The string from the balloons were suctioned to the top of his head, keeping it in place when he walked about.

"Well perhaps you could have been of use, had you been here!" Dorothy said.

"But then I couldn't have invented *this*," the Wizard said, holding out a small handheld device that had a large red button in the middle.

"Well what in the world is that doo hickey?" asked Scarecrow, who was always interested in the Wizard's inventions (even if he was often quite annoyed by the Wizard himself).

"Just a little thing-a-ma-jig," said the Wizard smugly. "Combining some technological mastery brought to you from the world fair of Omaha Nebraska and some magic home grown in our lovely land of Oz."

"What does it do?" the Tin Woodman demanded, no patience for this superfluous nonsense.

"A lock and bolt defying Wizardator, is the working title I have given it," the Wizard said.

Everyone stared.

"Well if I put the tiniest bit of pressure on this button here…" the Wizard said, pressing the large red button.

From behind them, the yellow door Mr. Teller and Mr. Story had disappeared through began to make strange clicking noises, then clearly the sound of a lock being released.

The door slowly, and just a fraction, opened.

"Why it opens doors," the Wizard said, smugly.

***

IT WAS THE SCARECROW WHO CHECKED THE YELLOW DOOR and indeed discovered it was no longer locked.

"Jolly, that's some invention!" he said, repressing his jealousy. He had spent his time following Dorothy's lead and the Wizard went and one upped him! And of course he had to put on this show, *look at me I'm such a great Wizard, don't forget who the best thinker in Oz is…*

"Well here you go," the Wizard said, stepping forward with a jolly step and placing the door opener in Dorothy's hand. "The lock and bolt defying Wizardator is now yours! Good luck…"

"What, wait?" Dorothy asked. "You must join us! This is our first step to escape this world, to understand what is happening!"

"Well, I do have the upmost confidence in the four of you, oh yes! After all, didn't you go on some of your most successful journeys as the exact quartet that stands before me?"

Scarecrow pulled the yellow door open just a fraction, trying to see what was on the other side. Lion finally pulled himself to his feet, unsure. The Tin Woodman leaned on his axe and observed.

The Wizard eyed them all, sensed a displeasure. It was times like this he liked to stand up straight, command attention! He arched his back, but unfortunately his head was not perfectly positioned above his body and he stumbled backward, the balloons keeping him aloft. He cleared his throat.

"This trip was made for the likes of heroes such as yourselves!" he proclaimed. "For in the face of danger after danger, whether it be by Witches, Nome Kings, Demons or Dirty Deed Doers, you have always soared like Enchanted Eaglets, thrived like Vining Vineyards, excelled like…"

"Wizard, is this going somewhere?" the Tin Woodman asked.

The Wizard dropped his jaw in annoyance. Then he shrugged, "Why do people use locks? To keep others from where they don't want them to be. Mr. Teller and Mr. Story used a series of locks because they very much do not want us to see what is on the other side of that yellow door. My guess is if they find one has seen it…well, they will be punished accordingly. And therefore..." The Wizard clamped his eyes shut.

The others were silent.

The Wizard opened his eyes and offered a wry smile. "So….don't get caught!"

He laughed at his own wit, then carefully maneuvered his body in a circle. He walked back into their new Oz, humming a happy tune.

"What a coward," Lion said, feeling a jealous pull. After all, it wasn't cowardly to want to be with the one you love in what might be your last day drawing breath. And the Hungry Tiger would still be suffering the trauma of nearly sinking to death.

Dorothy looked at the faces of her companions and gave a *humph* of determination. She knew they would dilly dally the day away. Dilly dalliers!

"You all follow my lead," she said, and she walked defiantly to the door that Scarecrow had been lingering around. She tried to peek through the narrow opening, then pulled the door open a little more.

Her heart was pounding in her chest but there was no sign of Mr. Teller or Mr. Story. No guards nor sentries lay in wait.

She looked back to the others expectantly. The gaze was enough, and they quickly (though grudgingly) lined up behind.

Dorothy, and the others, stepped through the door.

"Oh my goodness," Dorothy said.

"What...what is this place?" blurted out Lion, who clutched Dorothy's arm.

The Tin Woodman held his axe tightly—not because he saw any threat, but because the alien nature of everything he saw filled him with alarm. One naturally recoils from something that feels unreal, unnatural. *Wrong.*

Scarecrow was the most curious of the group, and a part of him was awed by the strangeness of his surroundings. He was also pleased the Wizard had not come, as now he had seen something beyond even the Wizard's understanding. He hoped he survived this trip so he could gloat—uh, *discuss* this with the Wizard.

"What is this," he said, his voice filled with wonderment.

The four of them found themselves in a huge spherical tube, stretching as far as the eye could see.

"I've never seen anything like it! Certainly not in Kansas!" cried Dorothy.

"It's all metal," Tin Woodman said, looking at the walls. He tapped his own chest and heard a clank, then did the same to the wall, which offered a similar, if more muted, sound.

"No windows!" Lion said, trying to get a glance of the outdoors to ease his troubled mind.

"And look at the lights," Dorothy said, at the blinking bulbs that littered the walls.

"And what…what's that sound?" Lion asked.

They all heard it; it was a low *whooshing* sound, coming in intervals like breath.

"It's mighty clean," Tin Woodman said, running a finger along the wall. The metal had a sharpness to it, like an electric current was within.

"Sterile is the word that comes to mind," said Scarecrow, proud of his vocabulary.

They had all been frozen by the alien nature of the giant cylinder, but Dorothy started to walk and the others followed. Dorothy's silver shoes clattered loudly on the ground, and Scarecrow's makeshift slippers squeaked.

"I've a feeling we're not in Oz anymore," Dorothy said.

They all walked down the circular tube, huddled close together. Scarecrow's little black eyes rolled over the blinking lights that surrounded them, making him think of little balls of fire. He gulped loudly, as fire was the only thing that could cause him pain. The Tin Woodman held his axe tight against his tin chest. Lion's four paws clicked against the metal floor beneath them, his claws extended.

"Look, a door!" Dorothy cried out.

They all stared. It had been about a hundred steps up, on the same side of the tunnel as their own door.

"It looks exactly the same," Scarecrow mused. "Except it is black! Could that be where Mr. Teller and Mr. Story are?"

"If it is, let's do this, once and for all," the Tin Woodman said, stepping toward the black door with his axe raised.

"Put that down," Dorothy rebuked. She held up the small box with the red button that the Wizard had provided.

"Let's think about this," Dorothy said. "Could it be an exit? Because what we really want is an exit, right? To leave this horrible place, to find the *real* Oz…especially before…" She shivered, thinking of the horrible scenes that had unfolded before them on the large screen.

"What's that?" Lion said, his ears pricking up sharply.

They were all silent.

"Oh I don't…" the Tin Woodman said but he cut himself off.

Then they all heard it.

After another cycle of the *whooshing* sound that the tube emitted every minute or so, they *all* heard footsteps…and more than one set.

"It's them, it's them!" Lion hissed.

"Let's kill them now," the Tin Woodman said, but softly and tentative.

More sounds floated down the tunnel toward them.

Dorothy, in the front as always, peered down the long cylinder. In the distance she saw at least two figures, though one appeared much smaller than the other, walking in their direction.

"I don't think it's them," she said, unsure.

"Well who else could it be?" Lion demanded.

"Guards," Scarecrow said immediately. "Other escapees. Minions. There are options, you know, if you actually *think*."

"The door," Dorothy said, taking charge. She pointed the Wizard's lock and bolt defying Wizardator at the black door and pressed the button.

The footsteps down the hall grew louder. And Lion had picked up the sound of someone speaking, muttering to himself.

"Someone's angry," he said.

"Guards, it must be guards!" Scarecrow said after weighing the probabilities.

Dorothy groaned in frustration and stepped closer to the black door, pressing the button.

This time she heard a series of bolts and locks tossed, and it slowly opened inward.

Now they all heard the echoes of the muttering bouncing down the hallway, and as Dorothy squinted she saw two figures, one tiny and one tall, coming toward them.

"*Follow me*," Dorothy said, and she rushed through the open door, her companions right behind.

They entered, shutting the door behind them.

They were breathing so hard that it took a moment for them to become thoroughly disorientated. As they gazed about the room they were knocked speechless. For it appeared they were in that same blah, dusty room they had left, despite they entering a clearly different colored door.

"How could that be," Dorothy said.

"This shithole," the Tin Woodman growled.

"Have we…gone nowhere?" Scarecrow said, shaking his head.

It was then that they realized they were not alone.

A man appeared, a rather handsome young man in Dorothy's eyes. Despite his pleasing appearance, he also looked haggard, like he had not slept or ate well in some time. And when he laid eyes on them he looked positively perplexed.

"Why…it can't be…creatures like you…exist…" He took a step toward them, paying no attention to Dorothy (despite she feeling like she looked quite attractive, to be honest, certainly more attractive to him than anyone else in her group, she would think!) and instead staring agape at Lion, Scarecrow and the Tin Woodman.

"What you staring at?" the Tin Woodman said, glaring.

The man was nonplussed by his hostilities, still grasping the shock of being in their presence. "Like on the screen…the bear and the pig and the other creatures…yet they talked, and thought, truly sentient beasts!"

"What'd you call me?" Lion demanded.

"Oh excuse me for staring," he said, trying to regain his composure. "But where I come from there are no creatures quite like you."

"Well you must come from a quite boring place!" Lion said.

"Wait, wait," Dorothy said, stepping forward. "Where I originally came from I certainly knew of no creatures like this. I grew up in Kansas!"

The man shook his head. "Kansas?"

"Oh, dear," Dorothy said. She had another thought. "America?"

Now the man responded. "Of course I am aware of that vile place! Why, an American. Here!"

Scarecrow looked about himself. "Where exactly is…here?"

Now a dark look passed over his face. "Ah. Sadly you are in a very, very bad place. My name is Jonathan Harker, and I implore you leave at once!"

***

DOROTHY LISTENED AS JONATHAN HARKER told a brief story of terror…and his terror began much earlier than when he awoke and he had been transported to this place.

"Just like us!" Dorothy exclaimed. "One day we were brought to a world like our own—like our own Oz. We woke up and we were there! And it was like our world, but *not* our world."

"Like our world but not our world, an apt way to put it, for a simple American," Jonathan Harker mused. "You see, I had lived surrounded by monsters, but I did not know how many existed! Not till now, that is." He looked over his shoulder, at the door and windows that separated this room from the rest of the world inhabited by the creatures behind the black door.

"Monsters," the Tin Woodman exhaled with a snort. "One or two chops with this will take care of them," he added, swinging his axe about.

Jonathan Harker gave him an unkind look, muttered a bit of profanity under his breath, then said, "They gathered us altogether, in this very room. Monsters, their creators...my Mina..." It took a moment for him to regain his composure. "And that was when they lowered the screen."

"The two men!" Dorothy cried out. "The horrible men, Mr. Story and Mr. Teller!"

Jonathan's eyes widened. "One with a mask, with lines and black dots?"

Dorothy nodded.

Jonathan Harker was nodding himself. "I did not know their names, but we saw them. After the butchering of the magical, talking creatures. And that small boy, his head exploding like ripe fruit." His shoulders spasmed as the vile memory resurfaced. Then he looked up. "They said the next competition is to take place for creatures from Oz! Is that…"

Dorothy looked down, upset.

"Ah, that is you," Jonathan mused.

"It is," Scarecrow said, curiosity helping override his fear. "Does your world have a name?"

Jonathan Harker gave him a gaze, but he quickly shook his head. "A name? I am from the world, the real world. And this is not a place for you to be, any of you. If you catch the attention of some who reside here, none of you will live to even see your battle. You must…"

"We will not go back till we understand what is happening!" Dorothy cried out. Then she stormed by Jonathan Harker. He reached at her, but she was fast and defiant and brushed by.

"I want to see your world," she said. "Because we need a place to…" She walked through a door in the back of the room, entering the world of Jonathan Harker, the 'real world'.

She grew silent, stunned.

"What?" Scarecrow asked, and he rushed forward to stand next to her. He recoiled in horror.

"Perhaps where you come from dreams come true," Jonathan Harker said, appearing beside them. He pointed out into the darkness. "Where I come from there are only nightmares."

Dorothy cringed, even pressed against him for a moment. It was the overwhelming darkness that stunned her; she did not think Oz had ever been so dark. The only brightness was a giant full moon in the sky that seemed far closer than she remembered it being when she was living on Auntie Em's farm. There were sounds too, an undercurrent of movement in distant brush, bats and dark birds taking flight, and wolves howling in the distance.

If Jonathan Harker recognized her sudden fear, he did not acknowledge.

"That is the Castle of Count Dracula," he said.

They looked into the night at the winding, weed ridden pathway that circled up the hill to the ominous castle that perched on the top of the peek. As they watched, lightning flashed behind it momentarily illuminating every horrific marble gargoyle and jagged edge that made up the castle. Dorothy recoiled at what could only be a giant lizard climbing down its side.

"And there, that pathway," Jonathan Harker said, gesturing again.

"It's even worse," Dorothy exhaled.

Cutting through a graveyard (though several of the graves had been dug up, and there were dead decaying bodies abandoned in various degrees of dismemberment lying on the surface, some of which had feral animals gnawing lazily at them) the path led to a second castle, one where tall bolts rose into the sky. Pulsating light passed from one bolt to the other, in such an angle it appeared to be a sinister smile.

"That is the laboratory of Dr. Frankenstein," Jonathan Harker explained. "He lives there with the Monster called Daemon, at least he did till it went mad. Now he is trying to create other monstrosities. And if you look at that swamp over there…"

He was cut off by a sound behind them, back in the room.

Jonathan Harker gasped and stepped back inside. He slowly surveyed the bare, dull room, a look of concern on his face. Dorothy exchanged a look of trepidation with Scarecrow and the two followed him back.

"Block the door, block the door!" Jonathan Harker said, panicked.

Neither of them responded, so Jonathan pushed through them and pulled the door shut and bolted it.

Lion, sensing his terror, began to smell the air, and a foul look crossed over his face.

"It is too late," Jonathan Harker said, "You have been detected."

"By whom?" Dorothy asked, and just then the door to the horrible world of Monsters swung back open, the heavy bolt snapping as if it was no more than a twig.

Jonathan Harker let out a small girlish scream, then quickly threw his hand to his mouth to stifle the cry. He stepped away from the door, though he kept shifting his gaze about as if not sure where an attack might come from.

Dorothy grabbed Scarecrow by one arm, and the Tin Woodman by the other. There was strength in numbers, she believed, and whatever walked through the door would find a fearsome bunch awaiting them!

A rustling sound made up of whispers and cries filled the room, growing louder and making Dorothy's skin stand on edge. Just when it seemed to become unbearable it came to an abrupt stop. For a moment there wasn't a sound to be heard in the world…and then *he* walked into the room.

Dorothy was prepared for something more horrible than she had ever seen, but what entered the room appeared to be a man. A tall, thin man, with thick long black hair, as black as the clothes he wore. His skin was white and his lips rich and red. His dark brown eyes surveyed the room with a detached disinterest, but when they settled on Lion, who was tensed with all his fur standing on edge, he offered a small smile.

"Ah," he said with a thick accent. He approached Lion, looking genuinely interested.

The growl in Lion's throat intensified.

"Oh kitty kitty," the man said, "there is no reason for such protestations." He bent down so his face was inches from Lion's.

Lion was still not having it. He pulled his lips back, showing his massive teeth.

The man snarled right back, and suddenly sharp, extended teeth appeared.

Lion's eyes widened for a moment but he did not back down, leaning forward.

The man burst into laughter and pulled back, leaving Lion momentarily confused.

"I like you," the man said, and he stepped back, even offering a small respectful bow. "Predator to predator. And you can talk, like the chubby bear on the screen."

Lion was still surprised by the encounter, but responded, "I can."

"Oh, hello?" Dorothy called out, curling at the bottom of her hair with her finger tips.

"Do not speak to Count Dracula," Jonathan Harker said. "He will put you under his spell, he will…"

"Count Dracula?" Dorothy stepped forward, offering a hand. "We are from the land of Oz. I am Dorothy, this is Lion. And here we have Scarecrow and the Tin Woodman…"

"You can call me Mr. Chopper," the Tin Woodman said, holding up his axe. He felt his own temperature raise ever so slightly.

"…and we were hoping you could join us to rise up against the horrible people who have imprisoned us, who are forcing us to fight and, and, and to kill!"

Dracula turned his gaze to Dorothy. It was bored, but at the same time she found herself unable to look away, and she relished that he was giving her attention.

"And why would I want to do that, silly girl?" he asked.

Dorothy was many things, but silly was not one. Especially when her life and the lives of her friends were at stake. "You're supposed to be a Count! I don't know what that is, but it sounds important. So you should know better!"

She pulled her gaze away (though it was not easy) and found herself looking at Jonathan Harker, who was quite pleased with that development. Seeing him though lowered her resolve; had she thought he handsome when she first saw him? Besides the silky black hair of Dracula and his long svelte body that seemed to flow like wind he was ghastly, really. Worse, it was like he was not even there.

Jonathan Harker saw this expression and he frowned. It helped build his courage. "Dracula, return to your castle! Leave us be!"

But now Dracula was slowly moving within the room. He approached Scarecrow, coming up quite close, his feeding brown eyes hitting the roadblock of Scarecrow's buttons.

"Hello," Scarecrow said.

"And you have life," Dracula replied.

"Well I do, I do," Scarecrow answered. He sorely wanted to find out more about this creature, both because of his own interests but also because of his want to gloat over the

Wizard. "A magical chalice brought me life. And you, were you brought to life too?"

"I *am* life!" Dracula roared, and outside lightning exploded and thunder shook and the room was so bright all had to shield their eyes, only catching a glimpse of the huge monstrous figure that stood where Dracula had a moment before.

"Okay, okay," Scarecrow said when the light and sound had faded. "You are life. Got it."

"Don't go picking on my friend Scarecrow," the Tin Woodman said, stepping forward, now irritated. "You heard your little companion over there. Go on back to your castle."

Dracula turned to him and for a moment his eyes shined with anger…but then settled, just as quickly.

"And you, look at you!" he said, waltzing over. "Why, is there even a drop of blood within you?" he reached forward and knocked against the Woodman's hollow chest, which made an echoing sound.

"Hey!" he replied, using the handle of his axe to push Dracula back.

Dracula rolled his eyes. "Not a drop. Worthless! So that leaves…us." In a step he towered over Dorothy.

"You leave her alone!" Jonathan Harker called, moving forward.

Dracula held her gaze and Dorothy felt herself melt into it. She knew that he would make her feel ways the Winkies never did.

"I do not think she wants to be left alone," Dracula purred gently. "It is early for a snack but perhaps…"

Dorothy almost turned her neck up, hoping to feel his hot tongue and cold sharp teeth nibble away, knowing she would feel vibrations of pleasure all over her body, especially her new favorite spot, the little special button between her legs she had never noticed when she had been in regular Oz (like, how had she missed that, right?). But then she thought of the horrible sights she had seen on the screen, and the way she only had a day to keep that from happening to her and all her friends.

She turned her neck away from him. "I was hoping…you could help. So we don't all kill each other because of those two horrible people!"

Dracula looked more amused than annoyed. He seemed to contemplate what was being proposed, then he shook his head. "That is not my place. And now, young Jonathan Harker, I will take your advice and retire to my castle. Until we meet again…"

He turned and started walking toward the back of the room.

Dorothy watched with frustration (both her special spot and the rest of her was feeling a bit underutilized at the moment) and she called out, "You could be next! They'll force you to kill each other!"

At the door Dracula looked back at her. He offered a pleasant enough smile. "My dear we are monsters," he said. "That is what we do."

Just then lightning burst so bright all clamped their eyes shut…and when they opened them, Count Dracula was gone.

***

ANY RELIEF (AND PASSING FRUSTRATION, FOR SOME) WAS SHORT

LIVED for even as Jonathan Harker was saying "Good riddance," Lion spun about, again a growl building in his throat.

"What is it?" Scarecrow said, turning his head. He saw nothing. "What do you see?"

"I see nothing," Lion growled. "But there is something here. I *smell* something."

"Oh dear," Jonathan Harker said, and he started throwing his arms about, as if punching an imaginary assailant. "Oh dear oh dear oh dear." After this proved fruitless he dropped his hands and cupped his privates. "Everyone watch your own. He has *no* boundaries!"

Dorothy and the others looked about themselves, confused. Only Lion had a more suspicious look to his large regal face. He tapped at the bow he wore on his head and sniffed the air.

"There is something…" he began.

But just then he was interrupted by a large banging on the side of Tin Woodman's hollow chest. It reverberated loudly through the room.

The blow had been unexpected, and while not with undue force the Tin Woodman still stumbled, which infuriated him. "Who did that?" he said, spinning around and seeing nothing, *"Who did that?"*

A low giggle was heard but nothing was seen, and a moment later Scarecrow tumbled to the ground when his feet were pulled out from under him. "Wha—" he said, spastically flailing his arms about.

"It's the Invisible Man," Jonathan Harker sighed, his hands still clutching his (not as small as you would think) genitalia. "His name is Griffin. He acts either with violence or foolishness, or somewhere in-between." Just then Jonathan Harker's pants were yanked down, though his under trousers remained in place. He looked at Dorothy and blushed sharply.

"Oh invisible is he?" Lion said with an annoyed growl. "Try to avoid *my* senses." He then exhaled loudly, preparing to take a deep breath and place the exact location of this pest named Griffin.

"*Stop*," Jonathan Harker shouted, but it was too late.

Just as Lion breathed in a huge breath, the Invisible Man released a musky smell in the air that had all covering their noses and gasping in disgust. Lion, who inhaled much of it, turned a shade of green and looked like he might faint. He turned to the side and gagged, some thick phlegm getting caught in his mouth and throat. He gasped and coughed several times, while the Invisible Man chuckled wildly, darting around the room.

"You…you…*bastard*," Lion managed to get out between coughs and hacks.

The Invisible Man was not shaken by the weak insult. One moment he was knocking on the Tin Woodman's head, another he was pulling stuffing out of Scarecrow's shirt. Then he focused on Dorothy.

"What do we have here," he whispered in Dorothy's ear from behind.

She felt her hairs stand on edge from revulsion as he slipped one hand over her right breast and gave a healthy squeeze while simultaneously thrusting a half erection against her ass.

"*Get your hands off me,*" she said, spinning and throwing a punch he was easily able to elude.

"He's bothering Dorothy!" Scarecrow shouted. "We have to protect her!"

Just then the Invisible Man again brushed his hand across her chest as he darted by, offering a small grunt which might have been a laugh but might have contained some gratification as well.

"Where is he?" Lion said, but being careful to not smell the lingering musk that soiled the air. He thrust a claw blindly. "I'll get him, he's mine!"

"No he's mine!" the Tin Woodman said, and now he was swinging his axe just as blindly. "Come take one step closer to Dorothy, go on and try it!"

Dorothy rolled her eyes. "Will you all shut up!" she demanded.

Everyone was so shocked by her tone they immediately froze in place…and Dorothy was able to hear the footsteps as Invisible approached from behind. Just as he reached around to get another feel Dorothy bit down on her lip, bursting it and releasing a jettison of blood. She spun around and flapped her lips, not unlike a horse, spraying blood spittle. It landed all across the Invisible Man's face; while there was no way to see his face and body, it was easy to see the splattering of blood that lingered in the middle of the room.

"There," she said bluntly.

Lion roared and with one leap knocked the Invisible Man to the ground. He lay there, stunned for a moment, before he started to crawl away, wiping desperately at his face.

The Tin Woodman approached with his axe perched but Dorothy stopped him.

"No," she said. She approached the crawling man, and with one swift kick to the gut had him lying on his back, moaning and holding his side.

"Pl-please," he said, lying on his back. "I was...I was just having a little fun..."

Dorothy looked down at the invisible figure before her, calculated where his organs might be, then drove her foot down. She estimated perfectly and soon had the Invisible Man's right testicle pinned between her foot and the floor.

"N-no..." the Invisible Man moaned.

Dorothy ground her foot into the floor until a small *pop*ping sound was heard. The Invisible Man screamed in pain as clotted blood leaked from the punctured teste.

"There's such a thing," Dorothy said slowly, "as *consent.*"

"Hurrah, Dorothy!" Scarecrow said.

Dorothy stepped back, saw the appreciative gazes from her comrades, and smiled, slightly blushing. "I think we have learned anything we can from this world," she said.

She turned away, wiping the bottom of her foot on the floor to clear it of invisible blood and mucous, then walked through the black door back into the hallway. Lion, Scarecrow, and the Tin Woodman followed.

Jonathan Harker watched, awed. He tried to think of the right thing to say, but it was only when the door was closed that he managed to yell out, "Well done my lady!" realizing full well he had fallen in love.

***

DANGER KEPT COMING, AS THE MOMENT they were back in the tubular hallway they realized immediately they were not alone.

"*Quiet*," Dorothy, now nursing a slight fat lip, hushed her companions, who tended to have heavier feet than she did (even with her silver slippers).

The hallway was straight so there were no corners to dart behind, but it was long and dark despite the rows of lights blinking on and off along the metallic walls. In the distance Dorothy saw the backs of two figures, speaking loudly and angrily.

"It's them!" she said softly, and she did not need to elaborate. It was Mr. Teller and Mr. Story, their captors.

"Let's go, let's go!" Lion said, grabbing at the others and pulling them back toward their own door, their own world. Oh, to be back in Oz, even an imitated version of one! Anything to be away from these terrible places they kept seeing. He tried to will them forward but no one shared his terror. He looked toward the yellow door, noting for the first time there were letters written on the wall above the blinking lights. He noticed a large **N** but was too distracted to try to make out any others. "Dorothy we need to go…"

"Hush," Dorothy said. "They don't know we are here. I want to hear them."

Lion groaned but Dorothy started to tip toe slowly down the hallway, Scarecrow following close behind. When they were near enough to make out what Mr. Teller was saying they lingered, pressed as tightly against the wall as they could go.

"…for your *own* good! You stay there until this process is done, do you understand? …What? Stop whining about that! You know why we cannot go outside!"

Dorothy stood on the tips of her toes, trying to see who Mr. Teller was lecturing. Whoever it was seemed to be putting up a bit of an argument because Mr. Teller continued to remain agitated.

"No! It is for your own good! Once we have rid ourselves of the competition everything will be different, but you must, you *must* stay in your place until all is completed! And as for you…"

With that statement Mr. Teller shifted his body and for the briefest of moments Dorothy was able to see who their captors were speaking to.

There were two people, and the first was a woman. At first Dorothy thought she was tied up, with spirals of rope going from her head to her feet. The woman blinked, and while Mr.

Teller and Mr. Story might not have caught sight of her, Dorothy knew she had been detected.

Their eyes linked, and Dorothy saw that the woman was not indeed wrapped in rope; in fact, for a moment she thought the woman had a giant yellow snake wrapped around the entirety of her body.

"Is that...her hair?" Scarecrow asked softly.

Dorothy did not respond but realized that in fact the woman had tremendously long hair, and that it was wrapped snugly around her torso all the way down each leg. She looked at the woman with the ridiculously long hair, scared for a moment she would reveal their presence. But the woman only looked away, a sad expression on her face.

Mr. Teller was still speaking to someone out of Dorothy's sight. "...and your name isn't the concern, so stop asking people..."

It was then that the Tin Woodman stumbled; he caught himself, but his axe scraped against the metal floor, emitting a loud, unpleasant squeaking sound.

Mr. Teller stopped speaking and spun around toward them. Mr. Story did as well, the black dots of his mask narrowing.

"*Run*," Dorothy said, turning and preparing to sprint down the hallway away from their captors.

Scarecrow's legs spun a bit and he couldn't get his momentum till Dorothy gave him a healthy shove. The four of them ran down the tunnel, aware that they were being pursued. Dorothy pulled out the lock and bolt defying Wizardator as she ran, slamming the red button as they approached the yellow door.

At first nothing happened, but just as Lion started scratching at it the locks and bolts started being thrown. Lion's full weight was on the door by this point and the moment the last infringement was lifted it opened inward and Lion's majestic body tumbled into the bare room. The Tin Woodman and Scarecrow pushed through, tumbling over the fallen beast. Dorothy was last, hurdling the massive pile up like an Olympian. Then she spun about.

"Close the door, close it!" she cried.

Lion rolled over and used his back legs to kick the door closed.

"They could come through at any moment!" Dorothy said, panicked that her companions were still crawling about attempting to get their bearings.

Her words spurred action. The Tin Woodman made it to his feet first, and he spun about.

"*Let those bastards come in, I will end this now,*" he hissed, the axe clutched against his chest.

Lion pulled himself to his feet and with one large step was positioned next to the door. "They can't write in their magic scroll if their arms have been ripped from their body," he growled.

They stood in tense silence for the door to open…but it did not. After several moments all exhaled, and in some degree of emotional exhaustion collapsed back to the ground.

Dorothy's mind was awhirl. How strange the world was behind that black door, that world of darkness and ghouls! She thought of that horrible Invisible Man and recalled with some satisfaction the way his testicle had popped under the weight of her foot.

But those creatures had been placed in that world, in as much as she and her companions had been placed in this one. Clearly Mr. Teller and Mr. Story were behind this, but why? And that strange tunnel outside her room, where were they located? And who was Mr. Teller speaking to, the woman with the incredibly long hair?

"Too many questions," she muttered to herself.

"What?" Scarecrow asked, as he made it to his feet and dusted himself off.

Dorothy shook off the lingering thoughts. She was about to say something else when Lion got up and walked toward the back of the room to exit into Oz.

"Where oh where are you going?" she asked.

"I'm going home to take a nap," Lion growled. "And to see my tiger. I haven't spoken to him since he almost was drowned in sinky sand!"

Dorothy's eyes opened wide. "But we have to discuss! We learned so much but know so little!"

"I know enough," Lion growled, and he pushed out and disappeared into the grassy world of Oz that had been created for them. Just breathing the Oz air lifted his crumbling spirits a tad, and he found it within himself to turn his slow walk to a moderate trot.

"Oh!" Dorothy claimed. "We need..."

"We need to ready for battle," the Tin Woodman said. "My axe needs sharpening and..."

"Tin Woodman!" Dorothy cried, shocked.

He barely gave her a glance. "We learned enough. That if we don't battle as they direct they have the power to make things very bad for us."

Dorothy thought of the right words to reply, and as they formed in her mind the Tin Woodman took the opportunity to follow Lion back into Oz.

"Scarecrow," Dorothy whined, frustrated.

But there was no satisfaction there either.

"Much to think on, much to think on!" he said, and he too followed the others out of the small room back into Oz. He hoped to find the Wizard, so he could openly ponder all that he had seen in front of him...while perhaps not sharing *all* that he had seen.

"Well this is unacceptable!" Dorothy said loudly, stomping her feet. She was not going to allow this to happen, to see her friends forced to kill each other. She would stop it!

But how?

Well Glinda always has so many answers she thought, and it was true! When the Nome King threatened them, when outsiders broke through magical walls (remember that giant beast with the tentacles that came out of the sky?) it was always Glinda who made sure that all were safe and the world moved on, as it should!

But when Dorothy made it to Glinda's tower she was disappointed with the response.

At least walking through Oz had rejuvenated her, as it had Lion, and by the time she had strolled down the Yellow Brick Road and veered south toward her castle she had great thoughts of an alliance that would shatter the hold Mr. Teller and Mr. Story had over them. Glinda always knew how to solve problems.

Her castle had been built upon a giant sprawling tree, and Dorothy entered the trunk and immediately found herself in an enchanted lift, as vines carried her to a large room. Little twigs that had sprouted legs ran about, diligently working for Glinda, who sat in the middle of the room in a throne made of thick green leaves, her burning red hair standing out.

"Glinda," Dorothy said, but when she stepped closer she paused. "Glinda?" she said again.

Glinda had been bent over a wooden table sniffing deeply. When she heard Dorothy's voice she sat up sharply, rubbing her nose. At first there was a moment of disorientation but then her eyes widened in excitement. "Ah! Ah! Ozma

Ozma, ah! Dorothy! We need to talk I have so much to say so much to say and so little time before it all goes down, down down down! Oh my Dorothy it is so good that you are here I have so much going through my mind, so much…”

"Why, yes," Dorothy said, confused. Glinda was always so composed. Now her red hair was thrown back in a wild manner instead of the neat, trimmed bun she always kept it in. And her skin, which was usually kept pearl white with magic and make-up, was natural and pink and she had splotches of (well, adorable) freckles on her nose.

"I have been thinking so much on what to do about tomorrow!" Glinda said and for the first time Dorothy felt hope.

"As have I! And I have explored the world outside the yellow door, where our captors reside! I went behind another door, the same kind but black as night, where there were strange and horrible beings!"

Glinda's eyes narrowed. "Tell me, girl. Everything you know. Now."

So Dorothy quickly recounted her adventures in the land of Monsters, and the strange tunnel that resided outside the door, and even the woman with the hair wrapped from head to toe around her body that she had seen.

Glinda listened, then nodded. "As I suspected, there is much at play. This strange new place is the tip of what is happening here…"

"This *horrible* place!" Dorothy interrupted.

"Oh, it is not all bad," Glinda said. She lay some white powder down on the table in front of her. "There is none of *this* in our Oz." She bent down, put a finger over one nostril, and snorted the powder before sitting up. "Oh oh, *Ozma*," she said, her eyes closed.

Dorothy watched, unsure.

Glinda had a slight sheen of sweat on her face and she spoke fast. "You see Dorothy, this, this magical powder makes everything so clear, *so clear*. And I see what I must do!"

"We must stop them!" Dorothy said, glancing at the table to see if any of the magical powder was left over.

Glinda was not in a sharing mood, and she quickly sniffed up the last of it. Then she spoke in one burst, "It has always been *me*, it has always been *I*, that has been in charge of keeping Oz afloat, of keeping the villains at bay, of ensuring the safety of our land, and that has not changed, oh no, that has not changed, and it will be I that will overcome Mr. Teller and Mr. Story, it will be I who must!"

Dorothy was nodding her head. To have some of the pressure taken off her, to be told that she would have someone fighting by her side, finally she felt progress could be made! And a powerful sorcerer like Glinda!

"What shall we do?" she asked. "Shall we call for a meeting?"

"What? A meeting? No!" Glinda snorted in laughter. "No, clearly it is I who must win the purging competition! Then

I will determine what needs to be done to bring Oz back to all its glory.”

Dorothy stared at her.

Glinda leapt from her throne and began to pace about, speaking more to herself. “Once I have disposed of everyone else I will find the true Oz…bringing this wonderful powder of course, of course…and I will find others to be leaders! Yes it is on me to keep the world of Oz alive and I will…all are expendable *except* Oz, Oz will live on, Oz must live on!”

Dorothy grew more frustrated with every uttered syllable and finally blurted out, “I am expendable? Scarecrow is expendable? Lion is expendable?”

Glinda stopped, almost shocked. “Well when you put it like that it sounds rather cold,” she replied. She thought for a moment. Then, a tense look still on her face, she nodded. “But in times of great trials it is sometimes a cold heart which must lead. Thank you, thank you Dorothy, for the information you have provided! I *thought* I might have to make the sacrifice of overseeing the extermination of the rest of the inhabitants of this little Oz, but you have reinforced it. Now I *know* I must. Hurrah for Dorothy!”

At that point all the small twigs which were still running about (some were carrying small platters holding more of the magical white power which Glinda eyed hungrily) paused and shouted with tiny mouths, “Hurrah for Dorothy!” before continuing on their missions.

Dorothy only stood and watched a short while longer, but as Glinda bent down for another healthy sniff of the white powder she decided it was time to take her leave.

***

DOROTHY WAS INDEED DOWNHEARTED as she walked across the land (which she noted seemed even smaller than when they first arrived in this already tiny imitation of their beloved Oz) and she stayed distraught till she made it to the palace on the outskirts of Emerald City where her apartment was in the South Tower.

Before she could even enter she encountered someone who was waiting for her.

"Hello Dorothy."

She spun in surprise. She *hated* that her heart was racing so fast. This was supposed to be Oz! This was supposed to be the Emerald City! Nothing bad was supposed to happen here.

The Tin Woodman, holding his axe on his shoulder, used his other hand to show he came in peace. "Hey, nothing has started yet, Dorothy. I just thought perhaps we should talk."

"What is there to talk about," Dorothy responded, truly despondent. "I have tried to speak to others and no one will listen."

"If you mean trying to keep people from taking part in this battle to the death...well yes, it appears our hands are tied by those dastardly villains." The Tin Woodman pretended to be in deep thought, then acted as if he had just come upon an idea, though it was one he had been carrying with him much of the day.

"But," he said, "What if the two of us made a decision that we would form a...let us call it, an alliance? For after all, what chance do you have against Lion, Tiger, even that beast roaming under the ground? But together..."

Dorothy stared agape. "You want to form a kind of...team?"

"Exactly! I knew you would understand. We..."

"Why that is *horrible*, just *horrible*, that you think we should plan to, to, to *murder* our friends!"

"It's not my game, I'm just playing by the rules," the Tin Woodman said, shrugging. "I just thought that with my axe by your side..."

Dorothy glared at him, angry. Angry that he would propose such a thing, and perhaps angry that he might be right. "Well tell me this," she said hotly. "You have your oh so mighty axe. A body of tin. What do I bring? Why would you want to team up with me?"

"Oh Dorothy," the Tin Woodman said leaning forward. "You're Ozma-damn *Dorothy Gale*. You're the center of it all. Of *course* I want to team up with you!"

Dorothy was a little taken aback by the strange flattery, but then she refocused. "And what happens when it is just the two of us? What happens to our 'alliance' then?"

He smiled and shrugged, "Well then it's everyone for themselves." He pretended to take a swing at her with his axe.

"No. *No!* That's, that's *horrible!*" She turned and pulled the door to her castle open.

"Think about it!" he called as she stormed up the stairs.

She felt her will drain even more. She wondered if others had approached each other, if others schemed like this. Could Scarecrow be speaking to Lion about the same arrangement? Or the Wicked Witch whispering in the Wizard's ear? The thought made her want to throw herself on her bed and weep. She ran the last few steps to her room and burst inside, but even the chance to cry her pain away on her enchanted sheets had been taken from her.

Someone had been in her home—perhaps it was Mr. Story, with his horrible striped face?—and they had left her something on her bed.

First there was thick leather armor. She sat at the edge of her bed feeling overwhelmed, but that did not stop her from picking up the individuals pieces of armor, for her head, her chest, her thighs, her arms. One by one, without even thinking, she slipped each of the pieces on. Each fit perfectly, and she felt stronger and more confident as the articles of protective clothing were strapped into place on her body. By the time she was done she felt stronger than she ever had, and almost wished there was a battle she could jump into.

There was more than just the armor, however.

There were several blades, some of which slipped into slots left open in the armor. She saw triggers which, with the smallest applications of pressure, would shoot the blades out at a deadly speed. There were also several other weapons, from machetes to various knives and even swords. She picked up each one, parried, thrusted. She put a particularly jagged blade into an imaginary assailant (in her mind it was the horrible Invisible Man) and pulled it up, dumping his innards out at his feet.

After a prolonged period of doing this she felt a moment of revulsion, so much so that she dropped the knife she had been holding and gave a little scream and kicking dance.

"I won't, I won't, *I won't*," she said, pacing back and forth. But Glinda's words went through her head and she wondered how she would react if some of the others—some of her friends—attempted to take arms to her.

It was a horrible thought, and assaulted by these ideas she lay down and fell into a restless, horrible sleep where she was being chased down the sterile tubular cylinder by first Mr. Story and Mr. Teller...but then, even worse, by Lion. By Scarecrow. By the Tin Woodman, waving his blood soaked axe.

She jerked awake and without even thinking her right hand grabbed the blade she had fallen asleep besides and thrust it in front of her.

Something feels different...

It did, and she couldn't place it. There was a current in the air, a nastiness. She sat up, looking around her room. She had slept, and dawn was creeping through her window.

"Hey...hey Dorothy, I'm coming for you."

The words came from outside. Dorothy slowly walked to the window and looked down; her room was about thirty feet off the ground.

It was still Oz, but now it was not only smaller. Now the kind pallor that typically hung over its landscapes was replaced with a strange darkness. All was thrust upon each other, so that none could run and hide. She gave a quick glance in all directions and saw the Yellow Brick Road was more path than road, the Forest of Great Beasts looked more like a grove, and she could see Castles that resided on the eastern tip and the western tip without turning her head.

"Dorothy...I've waited a long time for...this..."

Dorothy looked to the ground and the Nome King, one of her oldest and worst enemies, was at the bottom of her tower. He looked different than he usually did; while he was still short and had a long thick white beard, he now had two giant sharp teeth protruding from his mouth. He was also thicker across the chest, like he had developed muscles he did not previously have.

"You took my magic belt Dorothy," the Nome King said, his voice raspy from living in dirt. *"Now I will strangle you with it!"*

With that the King used his new teeth and drove them into the stone castle. They stuck. He then pulled himself up a few steps and grabbed the tower with his hands. He pulled his teeth free, then drove them into the stone higher up. He again used them to drag himself another step closer.

Dorothy moved away from the window, spun about. She went back to the bed and grabbed her jagged blade. She returned to the window. The Nome King was still making progress up the side of the building.

"Come up here, I'm ready," Dorothy shouted, her heart pounding.

The Nome King didn't respond, but continued to use his teeth as a pick.

Dorothy waited, planning to plunge the blade into the top of his head when it was within reach, when from the woods near the castle another appeared.

The tall lanky figure was instantly recognizable. His arms and legs were as thin as the sharp blade he held. His neck was long and slender, but strong enough to balance his pumpkin head. His nose and eyes were just cut outs from the original pumpkin, but now he had blazing red eyes behind the eye sockets. In the past when Dorothy had seen them they had always been kind, but now they burned with fury and insanity.

"Nome King!" he shouted, and he took his blade and let it fall to the ground at his feet. From his belt he pulled out several additional projectiles.

The Nome King had been ignoring him, but he yanked his teeth free, clutching at the stone with his hands, and looked back. *"I'll deal with you later Jack Pumpkinhead. Go fuck a squash."*

"Oh so verrrrrrry clever!" Jack Pumpkinhead responded. "You deserve a reward! A meal fit for a troooooll!" Then he began to throw the small balls through the air.

The first missed the Nome King but as it splattered against the rock beside him he saw what it was: Jack Pumpkinhead was throwing eggs at him.

"No!" he cried. *"That's cheating, that's poison! Wait till I..."*

But even as he shouted his objections the next egg struck him right between his shoulder blades, exploding yolk and albumen all over him.

"Stop!" the Nome King cried, losing his balance for one moment. He flailed his arms, then stuck his teeth back in the rock to steady himself.

This left his backside completely vulnerable to attack. Dorothy watched as Jack Pumpkinhead hurled egg after egg, each one striking the Nome King between his shoulder blades and his buttocks. Soon he was soaked in its poison (as all know Nome Kings are immortal...unless weakened by an egg) and he finally pulled his teeth free. He gripped the stone as best he could but he started to slide down the tower.

He looked back, his face flush with anger, *"I'll get you..."* he began, but then an egg struck him between the eyes, exploding in his face. He lost all grip on the tower and tumbled surely to his death, hitting the ground hard.

Dorothy despised the Nome King (a true enemy of Oz!) but she still offered a small gasp as the small king's body hit the surface and bounced several feet in the air, before hitting the ground and settling there, still blindly wiping at the eggy liquid that covered his face.

"You'll...pay...you'll..." he muttered trying to wipe his eyes clear, injured but still feisty.

Jack Pumpkinhead more danced than walked on his incredibly thin and long legs till he stood over the small squirming Nome King, who was still lying on his back. He frantically wiped the egg from his eyes and mouth, muttering curses and threats.

"Youuuu do not understand," Jack Pumpkinhead said, and he took the blade he held and thrust it forward into the Nome King's chest.

Dorothy gasped, throwing her hand to her mouth.

"Aghhhh," moaned the Nome King, putting his hands around the blade, even as Jack's pumpkin grin spread even wider as he dragged the knife down from the Nome King's chest to his stomach.

"Fun!" Jack said, and he pulled the dagger out and dropped it to the ground. He kicked it away and then reached into the Nome King's torso and pulled out a steaming pile of intestine links and gristle.

Spit and blood foamed from the Nome King's mouth; it was the eggs, he thought, as he felt a brutal tug of his internal organs being pulled free. It…was…the…eggs.

"Looook Dorothy, Looooook!" Jack Pumpkinhead said. He grabbed an end of the Nome King's small intestine (which was surprisingly long) and started to unravel it, pulling it out till he had several feet of sausage like links wrapped around his thin arms. As blood and bile dribbled down his pumpkin face he called out, "Catch, Dorrrothy, catch!" Then, like a lasso, he tossed one end of the small intestines up the tower while holding the other. It only went about halfway toward Dorothy, then hit the stone with a wet *splat*. It lingered there for a moment before the tip peeled back from the tower dangling.

Dorothy felt her mouth fill with vomit and barely got it open, where it spilled down the side of the building, some chunks hitting the dangling small intestine and sticking.

"Oooooooh, good one, Dorrothy!" Jack Pumpkinhead said dancing from one long skinny leg to the other, like he was doing a jig. "Now commmme down, I want to plaaaaay!"

Jack Pumpkinhead continued to hop from foot to foot and he started to make a high pitched whistle. Pumpkin seeds and flesh spewed from his mouth and landed in the Nome King's open torso and mixed with his white beard. In the distance the ground shook.

The sound was horrible and Dorothy covered her ears. She shook her head sobbing, and for some strange reason it occurred to her that others were watching this right now, on a giant screen, just like they had watched when the donkey had danced on the skull of the little child.

Jonathan Harker and that horrible Invisible Man and that so tasty Dracula are watching this now, and the thought filled her with some resolve. She would not have the Invisible Man seeing her so weak, not her!

She took her hands from her ears and looked back at her assortment of weapons…and that was when she heard the pained screaming from the ground below.

It was Jack Pumpkinhead. He was still doing a little jig over the disemboweled body of the fallen Nome King but now his hands were clutched to the sides of his pumpkin head, which was throbbing, like an inflamed blister.

"Dorothyyyyy, help meeeeee," he said, still holding his pulsating head which was rapidly losing its integrity.

Now Dorothy had always wondered (since the Powder of Life was used to bring him to life) if Jack's head and body were filled with blood and veins and bone like hers was, or if it was made up of just pumpkin seeds and pulp. Now she saw that it was a combination of both.

He was barely able to get a scream out before his head exploded, his eyes turning to liquid and shooting out of his pumpkin head before the rest exploded in a bloody, orange, pulpy mess, spraying the side of the tower a bright red and orange smear.

"What…" Dorothy whispered, and that was when she saw someone appear from the trees.

"Oh come now, what a mess," Glinda said, still waving her wand. As Dorothy watched she slipped it back into a waist band, then pulled a small bag from her pocket. She scooped out some powder and, hesitating only a moment on her approach, took a healthy snort of it. "Oh *yes,* oh *Ozma,*" she exclaimed, just as she looked up and saw Dorothy staring at her from the tower window.

"Oh hello sweet Dorothy," she said, tapping her feet impatiently on the ground. "Be a dear and come down so we can handle this quickly and, I hope, much *cleaner.* You of all people know what needs to be done. No reason to be messy about it."

"Leave me alone!" Dorothy called out.

"Tut tut, we mustn't lose our manners merely because we find ourselves fighting to the death. Now I could bring the entire castle down, but that surely seems to be overkill, don't you think?"

Dorothy felt overwhelmed, and it did not help when a moment later Glinda shot out a bolt from her wand that hit the stone alongside her window and caused it to crumble to dust.

"Come now," Glinda called. "There is no time for…"

She was cut off by a loud, ferocious roar, and was barely able to spin around when the Hungry Tiger leapt from the trees behind her and swiped at her with sharpened claws.

Dorothy gasped as she saw a cut appear across Glinda's back—not enough to kill, but certainly painful nonetheless. As Glinda spun about Dorothy saw the rip in her beautiful white gown, when blood as red as the hair on her head started to ooze out and run down her back.

"Come play with me," the Hungry Tiger said, pacing back and forth, low to the ground.

"Why, sneaking up on someone from behind?" Glinda said, assessing the damage even as she tried to level her wand at the huge tiger, the second largest cat in the land. "Isn't that Lion's job?"

The Hungry Tiger snarled and was just about to leap, when Glinda aimed her wand.

"Be careful Tiger!" Dorothy called from the window.

The warning was heeded, and rather than leap into harm's way, the Hungry Tiger rolled, got up and disappeared into the grove.

"Come back here kitty!" Glinda called. She only hesitated a second, giving the tower where Dorothy watched one more glance, before following the giant cat.

Dorothy stood at the window breathing hard. She had many thoughts, and none good. She entertained all her options before she decided she could not stay there. At a minimum Glinda would return, and if the Hungry Tiger did in fact dispose of Glinda and set his eyes on her he could easily swallow her in just a few bites!

She retreated to the bed and stocked up on the weapons that had been left for her. She made sure all the blades that fit snugly into her armor, ready to be popped out with just the right amount of pressure, were secured. Then she was able to place a long blade in a sheath that fit across her shoulder, and she carried a shorter, jagged dagger.

She exited the castle and walked down the Yellow Brick Road toward the valley. She just needed to find like-minded souls, those who would realize that nothing would be gained by giving in to their horrible captor's games! If she could just find the Scarecrow, and perhaps the Wizard. And Lion! Surely Lion would never hurt her!

There was a moment of trepidation when she felt the vibration from under the ground. She was not ready for that battle, and she prayed what was in the ground would stay in the ground. The vibration continued for a short time, shaking the world around her. Then it passed. She exhaled and continued on.

She made it to the valley in a brisk time, trying to clear a mind that was cluttered with thoughts. Horrible thoughts and images bombarded her, and she rushed, hoping to find some peace. When she entered the valley she was first exhilarated, then dismayed.

At first she saw Scarecrow, sitting in the road, appearing calm and contemplative.

This filled her heart with hope. Surely Scarecrow understood the error in all this, being one of the two best thinkers in all of Oz!

Her hope was shattered when she saw what Scarecrow was watching. Off the Yellow Brick Road the Tin Woodman was holding his axe menacingly as he paced about, Lion growling.

"Please stop!" she called, but no one heard. She began to run, just in time to see the Tin Woodman bring his axe down, missing Lion's head by inches.

Lion shot out a mighty paw and it struck the Tin Woodman's arm, sending him sprawling. He did not lose his grip on his axe though, and he was soon back on his feet, pacing.

"You forget Lion!" he called, holding the axe in front of him. "I've already been torn limb from limb. There's nothing you can do!"

Lion lowered his head to the ground as he walked. "I forget nothing," he growled. "I will swallow you piece by piece and part of you will reside in my gut and the rest in my shit."

"*Stop it!*" Dorothy shouted, with such fervor and pain and desperation that for a moment both warriors stopped and looked to her.

"This is what those horrible people want!" Dorothy continued. Tears of frustration and exertion ran down her face as she continued. *"We need to stop it! And we can! If we just stick together we can convince others not to fight!"*

Lion blinked, gave a suspicious look at the Tin Woodman, then looked back to Dorothy. "But they have that magic quill," he responded. "What can we do to counter that?"

"Yes!" the Tin Woodman added. "And if only one of us is able to live on, why shouldn't it be me, who has had so much pain! Why shouldn't I fight?"

"Oh you want to fight?" Lion said, turning back to him.

It was then that Scarecrow, in one chaotically clumsy maneuver, leapt to his feet. "Perhaps I have come up with a solution!" he cried. "For after all, am I not one of the best two thinkers in all of Oz?"

"One of, true," the Tin Woodman said softly.

He ignored it. But he did have the attention of the others. There was a brief distraction as a sound came from the thickest part of the grove behind them—perhaps Glinda, still bloodied and bloodying in battle?—but that passed and all the others gave Scarecrow their attention.

Scarecrow spoke, but to their surprise, he did not speak to them. Instead he looked to the sky as the words escaped his lipless mouth.

"I am talking to you, all who might be watching but especially the two of *you.*"

Dorothy gasped at the hate in the last word Scarecrow had cried. She had never heard him issue an utterance of anger or hate toward anyone, but the disdain in his voice was clear. It was equally clear who Scarecrow was speaking to: Mr. Teller and Mr. Story.

Scarecrow continued. "You order friends to harm each other, to kill each other! Why? For your amusement? For another reason? I don't know, but you are wrong, and I beg you to see the error in your ways!" Scarecrow took his blue hat off and held it in front of his chest. "But I have to tell you that not all will abide by your horrible game. By your horrible…fake world." He flung his arms about to show his disgust with the fake small Oz they had been relegated to. "So I will be the first to show my fellow Ozians—and anyone else out there who might be watching—that we do not have to play their game! And that I, Scarecrow, will *not* play their game!"

Then, he dropped his hat, to reveal a small packet in his hand.

"Scarecrow? What is that?" Dorothy called.

Scarecrow ignored the question, and instead smiled at his friends. "Lion, Tin Woodman, Dorothy. We have gone on many adventures together. I will not see the last one end where I raise a hand to any of you."

Then he flicked his hands together and suddenly a flame appeared.

"Scarecrow, *no*," Dorothy called. Fire was the only thing that could cause pain to Scarecrow, the only thing that could kill Scarecrow.

"Good bye my friends," Scarecrow said, and he brought the fire to his chest. Immediately his torso burst into flames, quickly spreading up and down his body.

"Scarecrow!" Lion said, taking a step in his direction but stopping. He might not be as flammable as the man of straw, but he was no friend to fire either.

Despite the obvious pain he was in Scarecrow continued to look at his associates, and he continued to keep a small smile on his face, until he crumbled to a ball of ash.

Dorothy's heart filled with pain; her dearest friend in all of Oz, reduced to a small pile of brown soot! But at the same time she felt an empowerment: for Scarecrow had done it! He had shown their horrible captors that they did indeed have their freedom, that they could escape from their horrible game!

Dorothy made a move to step forward, to make a grand announcement that Scarecrow had not ended his life in vain…when she realized she could not move.

She was frozen solid.

She was able to shift her eyes the slightest bit and saw that Lion and the Tin Woodman were equally locked in place. She did not know that not far away Glinda had been about to lay a killing blow to the Hungry Tiger but she also found herself fully paralyzed.   In fact, all on the surface of Oz found themselves completely motionless.

It did not seem to reach *below* the surface, and Dorothy distinctly heard some loud vibrations coming from beneath her feet. How far below, how far away? She could not tell, and before she could dwell on it a giant screen appeared in the sky. She felt herself turning toward it, and was unable to look away when those two horrible figures appeared on the screen looking down on them.

For a long moment the two giant faces stared. One masked, with black and white checkered lines and two black dots that revealed nothing. Worse, somehow, was the other, whose face gazed impassively at them.

Finally, Mr. Teller spoke. "Scarecrow has violated one of the rules. One must not take one's own life."

Dorothy tried hard and found she had a voice She spoke not for them to hear, but for those around her. "And what will they do to him now? He has made a sacrifice to show we are not at the whim of these barbarians! We can all show them, we can all..."

While she did not believe the faces on the screen could heed her words, they seemed to focus their attention on her.

"What can we do to him indeed," Mr. Teller said.

Mr. Story turned his head and seemed to whisper in his ear. The more he whispered, the more Mr. Teller nodded.

The longer it went on the more unease Dorothy felt, and it grew worse when they turned back to them…and Mr. Story pulled out his quill and began to furiously write.

"D-Dorothy," Lion called out. "What's he writing?"

Dorothy wanted to respond bravely, but in that instant all grew control of their bodies again. Dorothy (and the others) lurched forward as time continued to pass, and it took a moment for all to collect their bearings.

Lion regained balance first (perhaps because of his four legs), and as he fingered the bow in his mane he said, "What's happening to Scarecrow, Dorothy?"

The three of them stopped all thought and action and turned to the pile of ash that had been Scarecrow.

The ash was moving, and then it formed together. After a moment it began to stretch, and as it stretched it morphed. Before their eyes the ash became straw, the straw formed the shape of a man, the man became their dear friend Scarecrow.

"My goodness," Dorothy said.

Then there was a surge through the body of Scarecrow, and slowly, he opened his eyes.

"Scarecrow?" Dorothy said.

"Aye, it…it is me," he said, looking down at his hands in amazement. Then he looked back to Dorothy. "Does this mean I beat them, Dorothy? Does this mean…" As he spoke he continued to look at his hands, and he quieted as he saw a spark appear.

"Scarecrow," Lion said slowly.

"What..." Scarecrow was cut off when his hands burst into flames.

"*Scarecrow!*" Dorothy shouted, taking a small step toward him. She stopped, as he was suddenly engulfed in fire.

"*Help me, help me,*" Scarecrow shouted, his entire body in flames. He collapsed to the ground, screaming, until finally the fire had consumed all of him and he lay on the ground, burnt ash.

From the screen, Mr. Teller spoke. "Scarecrow will continue to regain his form and burn to death over and over. This agony will continue until only one of you draws breath. Only then will it stop."

They all stared at the screen as it slowly retracted into the sky.

And at that moment Scarecrow reformed in front of them. "Dorothy?" he said confused. "What's happening?" He took a step toward them and then squealed in alarm. "A spark, my hands!" A moment later his entire body was aflame, and somehow he made eye contact with Dorothy through his agony. "*Dorothy help me...*" and then he collapsed to burnt ash again...only to immediately begin to reform.

Just then, Lion roared in pain.

"Lion," Dorothy said turning to them. What had those horrible beings done now?

But no, this was the Tin Woodman. He had been noticeably quiet, and while it sickened him to turn his blade to his friends he was pragmatic, and after all he had been through it was easier for him than most to turn feelings off. As Dorothy and Lion had stared in horror at what had become of Scarecrow (who had just burnt to death again, screaming in agony...again) he had stepped forward and went for a kill shot at Lion.

Lion sensed it and reared back, though the axe made good contact into his back. Lion roared in pain and turned to him, fangs bared.

Let him bleed awhile the Tin Woodman thought, and pulled his axe free and charged into the trees, his tin clanking as he ran.

Dorothy watched in horror. Scarecrow had just reformed and was calling to her, calling for answers...before his words devolved into agonizing pain. Lion, wounded but not mortally, charged into the grove after the Tin Woodman. And Dorothy was, for the moment, alone.

***

GLINDA HAD BEEN ABOUT TO DELIVER A DEATH BLOW to the Hungry Tiger when the world around them, including the two of them, froze. Her wand was outstretched and the spell—one which would, ironically, turn the Hungry Tiger into a rock statue—was residing at the tip of the wand, as spells tend to do. And that was when Mr. Teller and Mr. Story appeared, freezing all while doling out punishment for Scarecrow.

Glinda and Hungry Tiger were forced to stare at each other, and this did not lessen their desire to end the other's life. And even Glinda, who was always quite confident and self-assured, felt a moment of unease looking at the feral rage and extended teeth in Tiger's mouth. She adjusted her gaze up to the screens, the only movement she could make, and watched as Mr. Teller spoke.

The announcement (about Scarecrow's flaunting of their rules and his subsequent punishment) was followed with she (and all around her) regaining their power of motion, but it took a moment for their equilibrium to return and she stumbled badly.

The Hungry Tiger, on his four legs, regained his balance much quicker and saw that Glinda was still flailing. He leapt forward and with a whack of one of his mighty front paws ripped the wand from Glinda's hand...in fact, he ripped much of her arm clear from her shoulder.

Glinda screamed as a jettison of blood shot out and her right arm dangled down on thin strands of meat. She stumbled back, her mind frantically working out a solution to the dilemma she found herself in. For she was Glinda, the one who negotiated the peace between the witches and the sorcerers and wizards of Oz! The one who kept holes into other worlds from opening in her universe, who battled creatures that could barely be comprehended by the other smaller minds of Oz! It was she and she alone who would win this battle, she and she alone who would bring about the survival and rebirth of Oz.

The blood loss weakening her, she fell to her knees. But she was not beat, she began to crawl toward the wand. She had another arm, did she not? First she would stop the bleeding and then she would turn this overgrown fucking kitty cat inside out. Yes, as she reached for the wand she saw it in her mind, she saw that victory was still hers to be had…when a giant paw appeared from nowhere and stepped on the wand, snapping it in half.

"*No*," she shouted.

"Oh yes," the Hungry Tiger said, and sank his teeth into the back of her neck.

He bit down, relishing in the warm salty blood running down his throat. Then he tossed her lifeless torso to and fro, listening to the squeaking sound her body made. He let go and her body flew through the air, landing stomach up. He then lunged on top of her and buried his teeth into her soft flesh, ripping free chunks of meat and chewing them down in huge bites.

Thoughts of all the babies he had wanted to eat over the years fueled his hunger (and indeed the sweet tender flesh of babies is the most delicious, with their bones not even hardened enough to resist more than a crunch between his teeth) and he dug in, ripping out her stomach and freeing her intestines, which spilled forward on either side of her.

The Hungry Tiger took nary a breath as he began to gobble these new delicacies, and he was so lost in his orgasmic meal that he hardly heard the sound of an approach.

He could not stop though, his body shaking with pleasure. Let whoever it might be put a quick end to his life, as long as it ended while he feasted on this final meal. It was hardly worth it to look up, but he did anyway.

A wave of shame shot through him when he saw it was Lion, his love. Their friendship in Oz had been a deep and true one, and they had stayed up many late nights speaking of dreams and passions and regrets. It was only here in this new Oz that they had been able to fulfil other needs for each other, physical pleasure that saw them pounding on each other's bodies for hours on end, till they would collapse, exhausted and covered in blood and semen. He could not have Lion see him like this; this could not be who he was.

To his shame he could not cease his feasting, despite the regret he felt, despite the horror he saw in Lion's eyes. He gobbled down some more of Glinda's intestines before he was finally able to stop.

Finally, blood soaked, he turned to Lion.

"I am no longer hungry," he said.

Lion was still.

Pieces of Glinda still hanging from his mouth and stuck in his teeth, the Hungry Tiger turned his head to expose his bare neck. "Please make it quick, my love."

Lion approached him and placed his large regal head against the Hungry Tiger's. They remained that way for several moments, one being rather than two, not a word thought or a sound uttered, just existing together in perfect happiness. Then Lion without warning ripped the Hungry Tiger's throat out.

Blood poured out into his face and he accepted it, not tasting a drop. He stepped back and saw that the Hungry Tiger had a moment of life left, and he offered Lion a small nod of thanks (though the neck had been so severed it almost caused his head to topple completely off). Then the Hungry Tiger fell to the ground. After a few seizure twitches he lay motionless.

"No," Lion whispered, stumbling back. In the distance he heard the Scarecrow screaming.

"**NO**," he roared, so loud the world seemed to shake, the world seemed to change, the world seemed to darken.

Lion turned away from the carnage, roaring in primitive fury. He fled out of this horrible grove and found himself back in the valley near the Yellow Brick Road, where he saw a girl. His mind had devolved to blood lust and hate but even in this fevered state he knew this was not just a creature to be mauled, but one who had a name. A name he knew: Dorothy.

"*Stand back, Lion,*" Dorothy said. Earlier she had thought that there was a way they could fight against the evil plans of their captors. Earlier she swore she would never raise a blade to one of her dearest friends.

But with Scarecrow screaming in agony not far away and with Lion soaked in blood, she knew there was no other choice. She thrust a blade back and forth in front of her, trying to keep the giant cat at bay.

Dorothy sensed she did not have the upper hand. Yes, she had the thick leather armor that she had been provided. Maybe it would withstand an initial assault, but looking at Lion's huge sharpened teeth she doubted it would last long. She thought about fleeing, of seeking higher ground by which she could implement an unexpected assault. But before she could make any evasive action Lion flew through the air, snarling.

Dorothy managed to get her left arm up and Lion brought his teeth down on it, squeezing. She tried to pull free but Lion held tight.

"*Lion*," Dorothy gasped in pain, and was sure she heard a small bone break under the pressure of the lion's jaws. She became certain her arm would be ripped from her body any moment. As her muscle and bone acquiesced to the lion's jaw she managed to pull free abandoning the armor in Lion's mouth, and she toppled on her back.

Lion leapt on top of her, pinning her small body beneath his huge one. Just then Scarecrow screamed again wildly, begging someone to help, screaming words and names until he was fully lost in the flames (again).

Dorothy did not even have the strength to bring up her armor for protection. She just started to say, "No no no," over and over, accepting her fate, ready to be done with it all. Mr. Teller had won. Mr. Story had won. She had nothing left.

To her surprise she did not feel Lion's teeth sink into her throat, or chest. She finally opened her eyes and saw Lion's huge eyes were filled with tears.

"Oh Dorothy," he said, tears like giant raindrops falling down on her face. "I'm sorry Dorothy, so sorry…"

Dorothy threw her arms around his giant mane and breathed deeply, remembering their many adventures that ended with them in this exact position, she inhaling his strong, feral scent. Then she managed to squeeze a button in her armor and out shot a blade, penetrating Lion's skull and brain.

Lion spasmed, blood, brain and piss pouring down. Then Lion collapsed down crushing much of the breath out of her.

"You always were a coward," she said.

I'm no coward Lion thought, his last thought.

Dorothy sighed heavily, and, with Scarecrow screaming in the background, she began to wriggle her way free.

***

DOROTHY WAS GOING THROUGH
THOSE SHE KNEW TO BE DEAD and those who still walked the land of Oz when from behind her she heard clanking footsteps. From within the grove appeared the Tin Woodman, holding a bloodied axe.

"Ah!" the Tin Woodman said, surveying the valley. "Good work, killing Lion. I did not think you had a chance."

Before Dorothy could respond (and she was going to tell him to have some bloody manners, Lion's bloody body was lying right there and he had been their bloody *friend*, didn't he remember?) Scarecrow let loose a scream, just as his hands burst into flames.

"Oh *shut the fuck up*," the Tin Woodman shouted back. He glared at Scarecrow till finally his straw face and throat were aflame and, for a short time, he could just collapse in mute agony. "'Fuck'. What a wonderful word," the Tin Woodman pondered. He took a step toward Dorothy.

Dorothy got into fighting position, grabbing a blade and holding it out in front of her.

The Tin Woodman held up his hands. "Peace, for a moment. An alliance, as I proposed to you already?"

Dorothy did not reply, but she looked at him, little of the love she had felt for him since they had first met in her eyes or heart.

"Maybe I'm listening," she said. "*Maybe.*"

The Tin Woodman clicked his heels together and offered the smallest of nods.

"Well?" Dorothy said. "What do you propose?"

"We take on whoever is left together. Once there are only the two of us...well at that point we see what happens, don't we? But this will maximize our chances of being there at the end."

"So we don't attack each other until we are the only two left?" Dorothy lowered her eyes. "How about you drop that axe?"

"Ah." The Tin Woodman seemed thoughtful, then said, "Here."

Dorothy's eyes opened wide as he held out the axe.

"You hold it," he insisted. "While we palaver."

Dorothy slowly reached forward with her uninjured right arm, aware that with a quick chop he could cut it free from the shoulder. But he turned it so the blade faced himself, and she took it by the handle and clutched it against her chest. It felt good and strong. Powerful.

The Tin Woodman watched the expression on her face. "It'll cut through tin," he said.

Thoughts went through her head, but in the end she said, "If we do this...alliance. What next?"

"First we share information," he said, not wanting to betray the moment of panic he felt when he saw the look of power cross Dorothy's face. "Knowing who is still out there is valuable."

She nodded. That made sense.

"Would you like to start?" he asked. "Seeing that I made the first step in giving you my axe?"

Dorothy only hesitated a second. "Jack Pumpkinhead and the Nome King are dead," she said.

He looked mildly surprised. "I suspected Jacky Pumpkins would bite it early…but the Nome King? You're sure? He didn't just go underground and avoid…" he finished the sentence with a gesture to the dirt below.

She nodded, remembering how Jack Pumpkinhead had bombarded him with eggs, then pulled his guts from his body, slapping them against the side of her tower.

"I couldn't be more sure," she said. "Lion, of course. And Scarecrow. I worry Glinda will be a formidable…"

"Dead," he interrupted.

It was Dorothy's turn to be surprised. "Glinda? No."

"Half of her is inside the Hungry Tiger." He stopped, and they waited as Scarecrow reanimated, screamed and begged for several moments, then turned to ash. "And he's dead too. Throat ripped out."

Dorothy hated that even as she felt saddened by the deaths of all her friends, she felt a little burst of glee with the news as well. There were less alive than she would have suspected!

"So left…"

"The Wicked Witch," he replied, "The Wizard. And of course, the beast in the ground."

They were silent for a moment, and Dorothy could feel the dirt beneath her feet rumble. It was from a great distance, however.

"So what is our next step?" she asked.

"I was staking out the Wicked Witch's home," the Tin Woodman replied. "She has been waiting it out, but has an army of wolves and bats standing guard. Once we get through them, she should be vulnerable.

"So I have planned it out," he continued. "You follow me. I will chop her heinous pets to bits and give you a free path. There is enchanted water nearby. You will carry a bucket inside and give her a drenching. You get her broom, and we use that to come up with a plan to take on the Wizard. How does that work?"

Dorothy's mind was spinning. She certainly had less reservations about taking on the Wicked Witch than the other amazing creatures of Oz who she considered close friends. But she wondered if the Tin Woodman would be able to clear a path for her to get a clean shot at the Witch so easily.

"I'll need my axe," he added.

She thought about it; it was possible the wolves would overpower the Tin Woodman, which would remove him from the equation. And if he was successful, then it would give her a very real shot to take out the Witch: without her minions and protectors she was really a weak old woman. She brought down a lion, she surely would be able to bring down a sickly old woman.

"Let's go," she said, handing him his axe.

The Tin Woodman gladly took it back (he never felt complete unless it was in his hand), and the two began trudging west toward the Witch's tower. They veered near Dorothy's home where the Tin Woodman was able to verify the deaths of Jack Pumpkinhead and the Nome King; Dorothy kept her gaze to the ground, especially when she noted that some of the Nome King's innards still stuck to the side of the tower, little flecks of her vomit still visible and clinging to it.

"Ah," the Tin Woodman said approvingly when he saw the carnage. As his own axe had once sliced off all of his extremities it was hard for him to be shaken by a little gore, especially when it was someone else's.

They walked on without word. As they approached the Wicked Witch's tower they found a small gathering of trees to hide behind. Looking toward the tower, Dorothy felt her heart sink. Literally dozens of wolves and bats resided outside the entry, some standing, some sitting. The wolves had teeth bared and were awaiting anyone fool enough to try to cross their path. The bats circling above them were at least three feet long.

There were also dozens of huge bats hanging from nearby trees, and while they seemed to be resting in the shade

Dorothy certainly took note of sharp claws and fangs protruding from their mouths. A few lay on the ground, ripped apart, as if one claimed the role of alpha and needed to show its power.

"This is hopeless," she said.

"There is a small underground stream a few feet beneath the surface of this tree," the Tin Woodman said kicking a tin foot against the base of the tree. "The water there is potent. While I take them out, you start digging."

Dorothy was confused, but the Tin Woodman opened up a chamber in his chest and pulled forth a small shovel and bucket. He placed them on the ground, then closed his chest.

"Start digging," he said. "Once I clear a pathway for you, carry the bucket up the stairs. I will keep any from pursuing you, but it will be on you to bring the water up the stairs and to douse her. I don't want to risk some splashing on me and rusting me up. Once we turn the Witch into pudding we discuss the Wizard."

Dorothy looked at him like he was crazy, but realized quickly that this plan worked to her advantage greatly. She would be safely hidden behind these trees while the wolves and bats would tear the Tin Woodman to pieces.

"You think I won't clear a pathway," the Tin Woodman said, clutching his axe against his chest. "You forget who I am. Just make sure you free up some water and have a bucket filled."

"I will be ready," Dorothy replied, and to prove her point she took the shovel and zealously began to dig into the soft dirt. She quickly heard the sound of running water under the ground.

The Tin Woodman watched, satisfied by her efforts.

"Right," he said, and he turned his attention to the tower, and the beasts that guarded its base. He stepped forward, his axe ready for use.

When Nick Chopper had been born he had been a happy child. His mother had worried he might be a little *too* happy. She knew that even within the kindly land of Oz there was cruelty and coldness, and she worried that he had a sensitive heart, one at risk of being badly broken.

Don't always be so happy she would say, as he skipped down the paths around their home. *For one day if you let your heart be too full of hope you will find it can be badly broken.*

Nick ignored her words, and one reason was his extraordinary skill with his axe. He was only complete when he held his axe in his hand, and all around Oz he quickly earned a reputation of being the most skilled axe man in the land. People came from all around, woodsmen, foresters, crafty types, even rivals, all seeking his magical work with his axe. And it just filled his heart more, for he was well respected and compensated for something he loved.

All changed when he met Nimmie, a munchkin maiden who became the love of his life. Nick's mother worried even more as she watched the way her son fell head over heels in love with her.

You'll break your heart she would say, and he would shrug her off: with his axe in one hand and Nimmie in the other, he had all anyone could possibly want. And his heart just grew larger and more full.

But Nimmie worked for the Wicked Witch, and when she told the Witch that she was leaving to live with her true love Nick Chopper the wicked nature of the Witch flared. The Wicked Witch enchanted Nick's axe and had it chop off each of his limbs. A local tinman replaced each of the limbs with one of tin.

The Wicked Witch intended to turn Nick into a hideous creature, one who could not be loved by anyone. But Nimmie's love for him was true, and she refused to turn away from him, even as his arms, and legs, and head, and chest were all replaced with stained metal.

And despite the unpleasantness, Nick did not lost his warm demeanor. He might be made of metal instead of flesh, but in one hand he had his axe and in the other Nimmie, and what more could he want?

You'll break your heart his mother warned, scared that with all her son had been through there would one day be a pain he would not be able to endure.

But with Nimmie by his side he plowed forward, happily…until one day the Wicked Witch came to visit him in the field, where he had been chopping wood.

I took your arms and your legs and your head and your chest, and still you are happy? she said, her green tongue darting over her snow white lips.

My Nimmie will always be by my side he replied. *So I will always be happy.*

The Wicked Witch then stepped forward and opened the metal box that was Nick Chopper's torso. She looked in and saw what the problem was.

Ah she said. *You have a heart far bigger than one should.*

Then she reached in and with one yank pulled it free.

Nick felt a pressure like he had never felt, and then watched as the Witch held up his beating heart.

This will do she said, and took a large bite. She smiled at him as she chewed on it, and swallowed.

He watched motionless as she took several more bites, until she had consumed the entire heart.

Now she said. *Be on your way, axe man.*

Clutching his axe in his hand, he returned to his home. But he was not the same; he did not smile or whistle as he went to the forests to work. And he turned away from Nimmie.

Please she begged.

But he just shrugged and walked away. Finally he said *somewhere out there my body parts might be pieced together. Perhaps that will love you. I do not.*

She left, perhaps to find those body parts, and he returned to his home, which was now a cold, distant place. He did tell his mother *you were wrong. My heart was not broken, as I now have no heart to break.*

These thoughts all crossed his mind as he approached the base of the Wicked Witch's tower. For this was the person who had taken all that from him. Who had taken his bouncing step, who had taken the whistle from his lips. And who had taken Nimmie.

The wolves—and there were at least thirty of them—and giant bats started to grow agitated. The wolves, many of them at least ten feet long, showed their sharp fangs, thick gobs of saliva oozing from blistered lips. Giant bats hung upside down, their small beady black eyes now open. Their thumb phalanges were as sharpened as the Tin Woodman's axe. They had small but sharp teeth, perfect for biting down and not letting go.

"Bite on this," the Tin Woodman said stepping forward clutching his axe. Over his shoulder he called, "Dorothy, you dig! These are *mine.*"

Then he charged forward, whooping in celebration and blood lust.

The wolves were fighting at the direction of the Wicked Witch, to whom she had dominion, and they charged forward as only a beast looking to protect and please their master will do.

The wolves were pack beasts and they moved as one animal. They descended on the Tin Woodman, teeth sharp enough to bend metal.

What they could not anticipate was the speed of the Tin Woodman's blade.

The axe flew through the air like a blur, its sharpened tip soon covered in bright red blood. The headless bodies of wolves flew everywhere, and the last spasms of life surged through their jaws as they opened and closed their mouths in hopes of doing the smallest bits of damage even as death throes took them.

Soon the Tin Woodman was coated from head to toe in blood, and with every swing of his mighty axe he felt a memory come back; memory of a small child named Nick Chopper who used to walk along the streams of Oz with a smile in his heart and a whistle in his soul. Whose mother was worried that he held too much joy, for there would be too far a fall when things turned (as they always did).

The bats descended on him even as the remaining wolves pinned themselves to the ground and lunged at his legs.

Nick picked up his tin feet and drove them down into the skulls of the wolves, easily shattering them and driving bits of skull fragments down into their mouths and lower jaws. As he stomped on them (and was he dancing, why yes, suddenly he was *dancing* on their ground up bits of skull and brain!) he swung his axe at the bats who swooped down and attempted to scratch at his eyes and bite at his throat to pull his head free.

Nick's joy rose and as his axe cut through the air and ripped bats and wolves in half he realized for the first time in so long he could *see* Nimmie's face. He could remember how she looked at him, he could remember what it was like to feel pride in himself because he saw the pride she had in him.

He let out a roar as the last of the wolves started to back off, aware that they needed to regroup if they had any chance of survival. He stormed at them so confidently that several staggered back. Before they even regained their footing he had sliced two in half, one's guts poured out into the face of the other who instinctively started swallowing them down despite the fact his own esophagus was currently not attached to anything and the chewed flesh fell from his throat back to the ground.

And what spurred this? What had brought such joy to his massacre, that he smiled widely even as he was soaked entirely in blood and bile? *Dorothy.* He realized it was *Dorothy* who spurred it!

In his mind he saw Dorothy's beautiful kind eyes, her small smile. It was a bit like Nimmie's but sharper, smarter…sexier?

The last of the wolves were cowering and he made short work of them, hacking them into bloody pulps even as he laughed and thought of how wonderful his time with Nimmie had been. The way she made him feel, the way they held each other. Dorothy was like that, kind and beautiful. And he felt something, in his chest. Something awaken.

With every whack his heart grew more and more. Soon he was just pounding dead flesh but he felt a joy he had not felt since the Witch had devoured his heart right in front of him.

But now it was back! And as he ripped bats out of the air with his bare metallic hands and bit their heads off he thought that if he could do anything for Dorothy he would do it. In fact, he would be true to his word…no, *more* than true to his word! He would stand by Dorothy's side while they disposed of all the remaining beings and then when there were the two of them left and no others he would gratefully kneel down by her side, the blood and innards of the others still dripping from his tin, and allow for her to swing his axe down across his neck. Yes, he would do that for her!

So much joy and loved surged through his growing heart that as he hacked and chopped he cried Dorothy's name out once, then again and again, for his love for her was giving him strength.

And as the bats that riddled the air became less and less dense his heart grew more and more until it was as large as it had been before the Witch had feasted on it. He felt a love and contentment he had not felt for a long time.

There were bodies strewn about, all torn to pieces, and only one bat lingered before him. He was the largest of the bats, and he gazed at him with black eyes that seemed to be in constant motion. Nick stared at them, first confused, and then feeling a small smile at the corner of his lips. There was something in this bat that reminded him of someone. The bat neared him but he felt no threat, and instead of attacking him it licked a healthy stream of blood off his face. Then it soared above him and flew off.

Nick was a bit stunned, and as he looked around himself he realized there were no creatures standing between them and the Witch.

I did it he thought, and he realized. No. *They* had done it. For without his love for Dorothy he never would have had the strength to do this.

"Dorothy!" he said excitedly. "I did it, we did it! Now we must climb and…"

He turned back to Dorothy, who clutched a bucket of water in her hands. Without hesitating she threw it directly into his chest, his arms. It splashed up into his face and ran down his legs.

It was indeed enchanted water as he suspected, and he immediately felt his body rust up.

"Dor-o-thy," he whispered, losing control of his arms; his bloodied axe dropped to the ground. He realized that she had betrayed him.

"*Dor-o-thy,*" he said again. "*Why?*"

She responded by taking a second bucket and throwing it into his chest.

He felt himself harden up, immobile. An overwhelming darkness filled him, just as his mother had warned him of so long ago. He managed to say, *"Dorothy…you…broke…my…heart…"* before he was totally still.

Dorothy picked up the axe. With a swing his head flew from his body and thick black oil spilled down to the bloodied ground below.

Dorothy looked at the decimated animals at her feet, then at the decapitated, lifeless body of the Tin Woodman, frozen in place.

"Why?" she finally said. "Because I *am* Ozma damn Dorothy."

***

DOROTHY REALIZED QUITE

QUICKLY that she would not be able to carry a heavy bucket of water up the many flights of stairs necessary to use against the Witch. She looked around herself at the valley full of death and knew that the Wicked Witch still had a trick up her sleeve; the Winged Monkeys, who were under her command because she possessed the Golden Cap. As long as she had the Golden Cap, the monkeys had to do as she directed.

Dorothy clutched the axe against her chest. It felt lively in her hand, as it had when she held it before, but she doubted she would have the same luck the Tin Woodman had when assaulting the bats and wolves. She certainly would be able to take out several monkeys…but the dozens that might be waiting for her?

She thought for a moment, sitting in the bloody field beside the rusted and still body of the Tin Woodman.

"Whatever am I to do?" she asked, the axe now lain across her lap.

She wished the Scarecrow was there (she did not, actually, as in the distance she heard the Scarecrow screaming at that exact moment, and she was thankful she was far to the west, so the sound was at least dulled).

She thought hard until a plan came to her mind. She walked through the piles of dead wolves, pushing back at their bloodied fur, in search of some whose flesh was lighter in complexion. When she found them she took the axe and shaved off all the matted fur. Then she carefully skinned them, removing patches of skin of about six inches high and six inches wide.

She then walked back to the underground stream she had dug up. She scooped up small puddles of water and placed them in the skin patches she had cut free. She then used drying bat blood (as strong as glue, she knew, and if one ever is in dire straits for an adhesive substance rip the head free of a bat and use the body as a twitching glue stick) to fasten the skin patches against her own skin, minute but distinctive amounts of water trapped within.

She took a deep breath. She walked across the field and picked up the axe. She had to do a small skip step to jump over the oil spill around the Tin Woodman's head, then she entered the Witch's tower.

She looked up the stairs, took a breath, and began to climb.

The axe was heavy and the staircase seemed to go on forever. She held the axe in front of her as she rounded turns, but no monkeys (or any other beasts) lurked in wait. As she walked her mind went to what she had just done and indeed she felt a twinge of regret; for after all hadn't the Tin Woodman offered an alliance? Hadn't she agreed?

But, as she trudged along one step after the other, she remembered how joyfully the Tin Woodman had been chopping away at the wolves and bats that enveloped him...and how there had been points when he had been even shouting out her name!

It was like he was pretending it was *she* that he was hacking away at! And there he was, dancing on the crushed skulls of the fallen beasts, still calling her name out, as if it was *her* head exploding brains out the side!

No, she could not second guess; she knew she had done the right thing. But as she walked the winding circular stairs, her legs throbbing and burning, her arms aching from the heaviness of the axe, doubt continued to creep in. And suddenly a thought occurred to her, one she had had before: just as she and her companions had watched as the residents of the 100 Acre Wood had torn each other to bits, perhaps she was being watched as well at that very moment.

"Listen," she cried out, holding out the bloodied axe. "I know there are others who are watching this! The next time it can be you! You, forced to fight and kill your friends, by those two horrible beings who call themselves Mr. Teller and Mr. Story.

"They can be stopped!" She spun around the small landing, hoping unseen cameras were broadcasting her words. *"Mr. Story has a magical quill. You must break it! You must..."* She felt overwhelmed for a moment, thinking of how poor Scarecrow had nobly tried to sacrifice himself to show that they could not be forced to fight...only to be tortured endlessly. For she knew that even as she stood in that staircase he was out there, burning alive, only to be brought back so he could be burnt alive again. And again! His greatest fear, his greatest pain, and he forced to live it over and over.

The sadness morphed to anger and she spoke quickly, in case they tried to curtail her speech. "If you are in a small plain room there will be a door there! Perhaps it is a bright color, for the one in my world is yellow. I and my companions..." She swallowed some words, as all those companions were now dead. "...I and my companions have *been through that door*. There is

136

a long, strange tunnel! And it leads to every other world Mr. Teller and Mr. Story are holding captive. Do you understand? *If you meet in the tunnel you can join forces!* You can use it to take the quill from Mr. Story, to break it in two!

"I met you, Jonathan Harker! And others from your world! You know of what I speak! All of you watching this, get to that tunnel. *Find them*! *Stop them!*"

She was breathing hard when she was done, but there was little gratification as she had no idea if her words were heard or echoed into oblivion. She *would* believe some heard, she would believe they would act on it! For she was Dorothy.

She continued up the stairs and finally made it to the top.

Outside the doorway to the Wicked Witch's room were two of her Winged Monkeys.

They looked at her, unsurprised. She certainly hadn't been quiet as she climbed the staircase.

They also didn't seem to have much energy. Both held large, thick butts that had smoke emanating off the tips. The area was particularly pungent, with the same smell that had surrounded the Witch when she had visited her. While Dorothy surely did not know their names, one wore a blue vest and one red, so Dorothy decided to refer to them as Blue and Red.

"Hey Dorothy," Blue said, taking a deep drag on his butt. He held it for a while, then slowly released.

"You're not supposed to be here, dude," Red said, breaking into a little chuckle.

"Well surely you know what is happening by now," Dorothy replied. "And I simply must see the Wicked Witch, and right now!"

Blue held up a hand. It took him a moment to get a cough under control but then he spoke. "Doesn't work that way. As long as the Witch has the gold hat thing, we follow her orders, blah blah blah. And right now, she's ordered us to not let you pass."

"Oh, that's ridiculous," Dorothy said, and she started to take a step toward the door.

Blue and Red immediately huddled their broad shoulders together and blocked her way.

"No. Entry." Blue gazed at her.

"Well this is so…" Dorothy was overwhelmed. She was aware that the Winged Monkeys had to obey all orders of whoever possessed that golden hat. "So you have to do whatever she says? Isn't that ridiculous? Who made up that stupid rule?"

Blue and Red exchanged the smallest of looks, then Red said, "Don't know don't care."

Blue looked thoughtful. "Wasn't it that lady? Her boyfriend got pushed in the river or something?"

Red and Blue looked at each other in deep thought, but somehow their eye contact caused them to fall into delirious laughter. After this subsided they turned their attention back to Dorothy, though giving no indication they would let her pass.

"Oh!" Dorothy kicked the ground in frustration. Would she have to raise the axe to them? Her arms were tired, and they did not look the least bit intimidated.

"Hey, it's not like we like it," Blue said, taking another hit, this time smaller. "It was one thing when we were in Oz. Now here, when she makes us service her, two at a time?" His shoulders shuddered in revulsion. "There are some things that shouldn't be green."

Dorothy offered a smallest of sympathetic smiles, though she was distracted for a moment looking at the broad shoulders and strong hands the Winged Monkeys offered. Then she refocused herself and had an idea.

"Oh!" she exclaimed in surprise. "You said that you were ordered not to let me pass, is that correct?"

"That is," Blue replied.

"But look." Dorothy took a step forward, so she hovered in their personal space. "Please, take a step back," she said.

Blue looked at Red, then shrugged. They both took a step backward.

"Now you see!" Dorothy said triumphantly. *"You didn't let me pass."*

"Hey that's right," Red said. He looked at Blue, then without waiting for a response, took another step backwards.

Blue eyed this all suspiciously, then shrugged. He joined Red, then looked back at Dorothy.

"And if you take just a few *little* more steps," Dorothy said, and she stepped forward as they stepped back.

Red seemed to find this quite an amusing game, and soon they had backtracked far enough that they were standing in the middle of the room of the Wicked Witch.

Dorothy triumphantly stood there as well, and she turned to the Witch with a smile on her face.

The Wicked Witch had just ingested a large lungful of smoke from her glass bong, and she blew it out with a look of disgust.

"You two fucking morons," she said, looking at Blue and Red through her one eye.

"But we didn't let her pass!" Red said, puffing his chest out in defiance.

Dorothy watched as the Wicked Witch sighed at this in resignation. The Witch then turned to the other Winged Monkeys in the room that gathered around her sofa throne (there were about two dozen) and said, "I order all of you to rip them apart. Franky, lead the charge."

Franky, the largest of the Winged Monkeys, stepped forward. "Sorry guys, gold hat and all," he said, then he moved on them.

Blue and Red had barely been able to stumble back, words of protest still pouring from Red's lips, when Franky and the other twenty or so monkeys fell upon them. Soon their arms and legs were ripped free and tossed across the room in an explosion of blood.

Dorothy cringed (they had, after all, helped her enter the room) but held her ground even as the monkeys pushed away from the mangled and partly eaten bodies of their comrades and turned their attention to her.

The Wicked Witch watched all this impassively. "You usually aren't this stupid," she said off handedly, placing her glass bong down. "Perhaps the Tin Woodman could challenge my army with that axe, but you? Monkeys, put an end to this girl. Eat her face of..."

"*Stop!*" Dorothy shouted, cutting her off.

The Winged Monkeys had been about to spring into action at the order but when it was curtailed in mid-sentence they hesitated. They leaned forward, teeth bared, but stopped and looked to the Witch.

"Glinda and I have a pact," Dorothy lied, "In order to assure *you* are not the final being from Oz she replaced my blood with water. If they tear me apart you will be soaked from head to toe!"

The Wicked Witch's green eyes, deep set against her bloodless white skin, narrowed and she leaned forward suspiciously. The monkeys did not attack, but they were rocking back and forth, unable to remain still, awaiting the conclusion of the order.

"Water for blood," the Witch said, rubbing her chin. "Franky, cut the twat."

Dorothy held her breath as the largest of the Winged Monkeys approached her. He followed the order but put little thought to it, slicing a sharpened nail across her arm.

Dorothy was able to adjust her body so that she was sliced across some of the wolf skin she had lay out atop her own.

The skin was quickly breached, and the water she had pocketed inside sprayed out into Franky's face.

He stepped back, wiping at himself, then he turned to the Witch. "It is water!" he said, as if amazed.

Now the Witch sat up in attention.

Dorothy pushed her chin out in defiance. "If I am attacked, I will flood this whole room!" she said.

"Cut her again," the Witch said.

This time Franky paid more attention and cut deeper toward the top of Dorothy's chest. She had to position herself carefully and pull back at the last moment ever so slightly, but again the nail connected with the wolf's flesh and not her own, and more water poured out.

The Witch, now satisfied, seemed to think for a moment. Then an idea came to her. "My special poison, cover me!"

Several of the monkeys retreated behind her, where many boxes and storage bins were stacked haphazardly. One rummaged through before appearing, clutching a small vial which seemed to contain a greenish powder.

"Now, now!" the Witch said, pounding the side of her throne.

The monkey carefully poured the powder out and it sprinkled down on the Witch. She held her position for a moment, then gave a vivid shake.

"It is quite a potent poison my dear twat," she said to Dorothy, her eyes still closed. "I have become immune to it but for anyone else who touches it…well, it kills you quickly, but not *too* quickly, so at least I get to enjoy the show. Blum? Come hug me. Show Dorothy what she has in store for her."

Blum, a smaller monkey who had been lingering in the back, only hesitated a moment before walking to the Witch and holding out his arms. The Witch stepped in and Blum rested his arms across her white skin, before stepping back. The Wicked Witch collapsed back into her throne and gazed at Blum through green blood shot eyes.

All the other monkeys watched, giving Blum space. He stood in the middle of the room, and for several moments nothing happened. Then Blum started to make high pitched cackling sounds.

Well this isn't so bad Dorothy thought, but that was before Blum started bouncing from one foot to the other. His skin started bubbling up and he grabbed at it, ripping it free from his body. Soon he was dribbling parts of himself down in a puddle, screaming and gargling. Then moments later he was just a furry bloody puddle.

"Elly, Bammy, eat that," the Wicked Witch said, and two of the other monkeys greedily descended on the mess, slurping and gobbling what was left of Blum away.

"Oh my," Dorothy said.

The Wicked Witch watched with the slightest bit of interest, wondering if any good parts would be left over for her to have a taste. When none were (as Elly and Bammy were quite thorough in their clean up) she looked away, bored.

"Bring Dorothy to me," she said, holding out her arms, waiting to give a big hug. "I want to hold her tight."

The Winged Monkeys all turned their attention to Dorothy.

A panic surged through her; she did not want to wind up a puddle on the floor! So she dashed forward, swinging the axe wildly.

This was not unexpected by the Witch, though her reflexes were greatly stunted by the amount she had been smoking over the course of her time in new Oz (and why wasn't this around in old Oz? If it was she might have just spent more time in her home relaxing with it, rather than out causing mischief!).

She ducked and moved her still flexible body beneath her throne in one fluid movement. Dorothy and her axe flew awkwardly by, and she tumbled into the series of boxes and bins that lay behind it, upending them and leaving them quite the mess.

"Get her!" Dorothy heard the Witch cry, as she scrambled on the ground, trying to regain her balance and locate the axe, which she had dropped amidst the bins.

But then she paused, even as the monkeys neared, because she thought *why would the Witch be panicked now, she seems to have me as a cat has a mouse*!

So instead of looking for the axe she started pushing some of the items about that had been knocked askew by her tumble. She was still pulling and pushing at items when she felt the monkey's strong hands reaching for her, and when she saw what she needed it was just out of her reach. She lunged forward and just as the monkeys grabbed her ankles and started pulling her back into the center of the room she grasped it.

"All right, all right," the Wicked Witch, back on her throne, said. "Enough of your shenanigans, my little twat. Monkeys, bring her to me."

"*Stop*," Dorothy said with such force the monkeys hesitated, unsure.

"Monkeys, you have an order!" the Wicked Witch said sharply.

"You *no longer* have to take her orders!" Dorothy cried out, and she held up what she had found whilst scrambling behind the throne.

It was the Golden Cap! And it was the owner of said hat that the Winged Monkeys had to obey!

"No!" the Witch said, sitting up, a look of horror on her face.

"Dorothy!" Franky, the largest of the monkeys said. "We are now servants to you! Whatever you ask us to do, we shall!"

Dorothy was momentarily distracted by all the possibilities that went through her head. But then she shook these out as she recalled the gravity of her situation.

"Eat her face off," she said, gesturing to the Wicked Witch.

"No. N-no!" the Witch cried, knocking her own throne down as she pulled away. "You can't do that, you can't...*AHHHHHH*!"

The Witch's words devolved into an agonized cry as the first series of monkeys descended on her, ripping at the bloodless skin around her face and pulling it off, gobbling it down and then working on the thinnest, bitterest of meats that lay beneath.

The poison on the Witch's skin started to act on the first monkeys and even as they ripped at her flesh they began to liquify, pouring their own weakened and softened skin and bones on top of her.

Beneath the gurgling mess Dorothy could still hear the screams of the Witch, so she said, "Just kill her already!" and another series of monkeys jumped right onto the mixture of liquid monkey flesh and green Witch blood. As this group ripped through and tore the Witch to pieces they too began to lose their bodily integrity at the hands of the Witch's poison. The third batch of monkeys were able to finally tear what was left of the Witch to pieces.

Dorothy watched, feeling her stomach turn from the nastiness of it all. Once the killing frenzy had finished the remaining monkeys lingered about, unsure. When Dorothy did not give any immediate directions several made for a window, and took off into the sky.

Franky, the largest and the leader of the Winged Monkeys (or so it seemed to Dorothy), lingered behind. After surveying how many monkeys had been lost he sighed and turned to Dorothy.

"So we are now under your control," he said.

"Oh, I don't want that," Dorothy said, and she held out the Golden Cap.

Franky was shocked. "Are you…are you sure? You give us our freedom?"

"I don't want it," Dorothy said simply.

Franky took it. He held the hat to his chest, thinking of all the horrible deeds he and his kind had been made to do in the old Oz because of the curse of this golden hat. He wondered if this world was better after all.

Before he took flight to follow his brethren he looked back at Dorothy.

"And what will you do now?" he asked.

Dorothy only hesitated a moment. "I'm off to see the Wizard," she said.

"Ah." Franky looked in thought. "The Wonderful Wizard of Oz?"

"Yes," Dorothy replied. "That motherfucker."

***

THE WONDERFUL WIZARD OF OZ had watched much of the battle between Dorothy and the Wicked Witch with some curiosity and with great interest. He had known in his smallest of hearts that Dorothy would come out on top; the Wicked Witch was just too vain, lazy, and stupid to defeat her. He admitted he had begun to doubt, as he watched. But in the end he was not surprised when Dorothy had come out victorious.

From inside his small hidden fortress, he sighed (in fact, he resided in a hollowed out tree. It was useful and none would find him...until that beast in the ground resurfaced. That creature would have no problem sniffing him out and exposing his hiding spot. But that was a problem for later).

Ever since he had seen those screens descend from the ceiling and he had watched the carnage in the 100 Acre Wood he had set to work, using his knowledge of technology and magic, to create his own screens and to tap into the circuits used by Mr. Teller and Mr. Story. It had not taken long, and he had spent most of the time while others battled watching the battles, letting them foolishly thin the ranks before he stepped forward and killed the injured and mangled survivors.

He had just watched the conclusion of Dorothy and the Witch, but before he turned his screens off he turned his attention back to the large valley, where Scarecrow had just been recreated. He watched with glee as Scarecrow took a few haggard steps before first his hands, then the rest of him burst into flames. He chuckled as Scarecrow was totally lost in the conflagration, screaming in agony.

"And fuck *you* Mr. Scarecrow," he said, laughing as he descended into an agonizing death. *One of the two best thinkers in Oz my ass* he thought. *"I'm smarter than you, you bag full of stuffing!"* he shouted, then burst into laughter. It eventually dried and, with the smallest bit of regret, he flipped that screen off. He would check it out a few more times before he faced Dorothy.

Ah. Dorothy.

So you think you can defeat her without our chair?

That question had been posed to him earlier in the day, before even the Nome King and Jack Pumpkinhead had succumbed to the battle.

He had been working on another project, tucked away in his hidden hollowed out tree, when he heard footsteps approach him.

He had been stunned; could someone have already found him, someone who *didn't* live in the ground? Had he been lax in his preparation, had he left clues? If it was Scarecrow who walked in he would be most irritated, that was for sure.

It was not Scarecrow who entered, but he was not pleased with his guest.

It was the thoroughly odious Mr. Teller who had appeared in his hidden home.

Do not ask me how I was able to locate you, do not bother your little brain, Mr. Teller had said.

This ticked the Wizard off, but he would not let his annoyance be palpable.

As there are rules at play I do not yet understand, I will not waste my time at guessing he replied, unsure if Mr. Teller had come as friend or foe.

Probably for the best Mr. Teller stated, looking about himself at the makeshift lab and working space the Wizard had concocted. While the Wizard was proud of it and hoped to see Mr. Teller was equally impressed, he saw no expression on the man's strange, homely face.

And to what do I owe the pleasure the Wizard finally asked, frustrated.

I see you have little patience. That is all right. You will see this is worth your while. Here.

With that Mr. Teller had offered the Wizard a small hand held control with a button in the middle.

The Wizard was unsure if this was some kind of retribution for his invention of the lock and bolt defying

Wizardator (as it looked much like his own creation) so he was tentative in claiming the item.

Stop that Mr. Teller chided. *We are giving you a little...boost. Go. Press the button.*

Thinking of no way to stall the matter, the Wizard pressed the button in the middle of the remote...and immediately heard a *whirring* sound. Then a wheeled chair appeared in his abode, and, driven by an unseen force, it circled around the Wizard and pushed under him, so he was now sitting in it.

What is this? he asked, unsure.

Ah, Mr. Teller said with a joyless grin. *This is your little boost. Something to assure you beating that pain in the ass, Dorothy.*

The Wizard had been a bit stunned. He was displeased that they thought he needed assistance (he had discovered something marvelous while working in his station, and planned to use it to break Dorothy's mind before ending her life), but at the same time he was intrigued. He placed his hands over the arm supports and found buttons. He pressed one on the right...and immediately several gun barrels sprung up.

We will deactivate that for now Mr. Teller said quickly. *But come the start of the battling, they will be operational and armed, I assure you. Now lean your head back.*

Now the Wizard was always sensitive about his head. While proud of his huge brain, he knew he was at the whim of the balloons, suctioned to the top of his skull, that kept his oversized crown from drooping to either side.

But still, he was now curious, and he leaned his head back. Immediately he felt the smallest of pinches at the base of his skull, where the suctions attached.

We were worried that Dorothy might try to cut those strings and leave you vulnerable Mr. Teller explained. *Now the strings are uncuttable.*

The Wizard did not like to acknowledge this was a good idea, but he had thought of this vulnerability.

Not bad he said.

Now press the button on your left side Mr. Teller said, clearly excited.

The Wizard did, and several sharp knives popped out all around the entirety of the chair.

In case someone gets too close to you Mr. Teller said with a chuckle.

Why the Wizard had asked. *Why are you giving me all this…assistance?*

For the first time Mr. Teller seemed hesitant to reply, and his general smugness was replaced with discomfort. Then he finally said *Dorothy has a level of notoriety we are not comfortable with. We have a strong preference it not be her who moves on to the next round.*

The Wizard had invented his own small portable screen and had tapped into something totally different than the screens within the new Oz and the world around it. Scrolling through that, he had discovered something about Dorothy that made him understand, at least a little, what Mr. Teller was talking about. At the same time he planned to use this same thing to bring about her downfall.

Well I thank you for your...gift he said. *But I believe I will be able to dispose of Dorothy upon my own merits.*

Mr. Teller had raised an eyebrow. *Your own merits. Something more than green tinted glasses, I hope?*

The Wizard reddened a bit, and did not reply.

Mr. Teller grew thoughtful. *You think you can defeat her without our chair?*

The Wizard looked down at the remote in his hand, and deftly placed it into his pocket. *How about I keep it as a Plan B?*

Mr. Teller had left soon thereafter, and the Wizard had taken to watching the events unfold on the screens around him (taking particular joy in Scarecrow's repeated agonizing fate).

Now Dorothy had just defeated the Wicked Witch and was exiting her castle.

And walking right toward him.

The Wizard sighed. It was time to stop hiding.

With the remote control provided by Mr. Teller still in his pocket, and with his portable screen in his hand (he had called it a Wizard Portable Screen-ulator, but when searching through it he had come across the term 'tablet' and realized it appropriately described his invention), the Wizard emerged into the valley.

The moment he stepped outside into the sun he became aware of how loud Scarecrow was, despite being on the opposite side of the valley.

"Oh do *shut up*," he called out, repositioning the suctions on his head to make sure they were all secure. Then he reached to his sides and adjusted the levers to release a little more helium into the balloons that kept his head afloat, making sure they were optimally filled. It was wonderful having such a huge brain, but frustrating the way his head needed constant support. Perhaps when this was over he would utilize the new magic and technology he had learned and come up with a more efficient way to keep his head balanced and upright.

But! But first things first! And the current *first* was the sudden sound of banging beneath the ground, shaking the dirt beneath him so greatly the Wizard stumbled for a moment.

"Not now you beast!" the Wizard said, and he stomped the ground as best he could.

Instead of retreating, the banging beneath the dirt increased in volume and intensity and for a brief moment the Wizard was scared the land beneath him would open up and the snarling beast would appear.

He felt a moment of panic (though the remote in his pocket gave him some reassurance) but then he stomped the ground again.

This time the banging lessened, and the Wizard sighed in relief.

"How far away?"

The Wizard spun about.

Dorothy, covered in blood and still clutching the Tin Woodman's axe, stood before him.

"How far away?" Dorothy repeated. "Because we can't battle each other if he decides to surface."

The Wizard offered a jolly smile. "He has retreated deeper I would say, and who says we have to battle my dear Dorothy?"

Dorothy showed no indication of succumbing to his charms. "You can cut the shit, Wizard. I know you well enough. You already think you have outsmarted me. You haven't. I have been through too much to stop now."

"Slow down, slow down!" the Wizard said, and he did feel the slightest of unease. Dorothy was strong willed and smarter than most of the female persuasion (but not that smart, obviously) but she rarely was so *decisive*. And clearly she had decided this would be completed at the end of her axe. What if he wasn't able to get the tablet into her hands? What if he wasn't able to show her what he needed to show her to indeed break her brain into a million pieces?

Dorothy went to respond but Scarecrow let loose an agonizing scream, louder. She waited a moment, but before she could speak the Wizard was holding something toward her.

"Might I ask you to just look at one small thing?" he asked. "A little invention of my own?"

"You think I'm a fool?" Dorothy asked, stepping forward. "I have already been threatened with wild animals, poison, blades. What will *that* do? Explode in a fiery ball? Pulse magic through me that will turn my bones into worms? Why would I fall for that?"

"No no," the Wizard said, panicked. He could drop the tablet and pull the remote from his pocket but he needed to keep his composure. If he could just get her to look at the tablet he could beat her, he could pluck the axe from her hand and drive it right through her chest while she was still trying to orient herself.

"Look!" he said, holding up the tablet.

Dorothy was suspicious, but most of all she was tired. Tired of the horrors she had been subjected to. Tired of the screaming (and there was Scarecrow, even louder, right on cue). And most of all, tired of being forced to fight those she had spent so many years loving.

But the tablet did catch her eye. Because there was a picture of a person on it, a person that looked very much like…

"What is this," she said, her voice filled with awe and confusion.

"Look," the Wizard said greedily. "Take it. Scroll through it."

Dorothy held the axe in her weakened left hand and tentatively reached forward with her right. She looked at the tablet, confused. "Who is this?" she said, her voice small.

"If you push the screen you will see more. Do it. Do it, Dorothy, and understand!"

Dorothy dug the axe into the ground and took the tablet in both hands. She tentatively reached forward with her right index finger and pushed it. Another picture appeared on the screen in front of her. Then another. And another. And they all were...

"Why do they all look like me?" she asked. *"Why are all these people named Dorothy?"*

"Because you are one of many Dorothys," the Wizard said smugly, inching forward so he could reach for the axe. *"You are not special.* They are a little different but they are all the same, in the end. *They are all Dorothys.* You are not the one. You are not anything."

"But...but no...but...I don't understand..." She continued to scroll through the tablet.

And it was not just her. There were crude and haphazard drawings of people who looked like her, surrounded by a Lion, a Scarecrow (on cue: scream), and a Tin Woodman. They all looked a little different but they all said the same thing: Dorothy walking the Yellow Brick Road, Dorothy entering Emerald City, Dorothy's house ripped from Kansas and flying through the air, to land in Oz...

"What is this...I don't...I don't..." her voice fluctuated greatly. An intense pain filled her head. The world was melting all around her, and with every new picture she scrolled through the pain just grew sharper. "Who the *fuck* is Judy Garland?"

The Wizard saw the way her eyes grew more and more wild as she turned one screen into the next. The moment that he sensed she was fully vulnerable he lunged forward to grab the axe.

He had misjudged its heft though, and instead of getting it and slicing it through her in one fluid movement he barely was able to get it above her knees. He tried to swing it but lost his grip and the side of the axe knocked against her leg harmlessly, barely able to leave a scrape.

Dorothy's eyes were wild and her mind was racing. She understood none of this; *she* was Dorothy! She was the only Dorothy, she was the one who spread such love and goodness throughout Oz! These pictures...they were a fake, a trick...they were...

It was then that she felt the side of the axe hit her and she was able to pull her eyes free from the screen and see the Wizard standing before her guiltily clutching the handle of the axe.

"This is a *trick*," Dorothy said, and she smashed the tablet across the side of the Wizard's huge head.

The Wizard took the brunt of the blow directly, and staggered back, stunned, dropping the axe. He also reached up to make sure the shards of broken glass from the tablet hadn't severed any of the strings that kept his balloons attached to his head.

He pulled his hand back; it was bloodied, but the strings were still unmolested.

"It's a lie, a lie a lie," Dorothy was shouting.

"No," the Wizard said, still trying to get his bearings. "It's real. *They're* real. People post them..."

"People post *lies!*" Dorothy shouted, and she became aware that the Wizard was still injured from the initial blow. She dropped the broken tablet filled with lies to the ground and grabbed her axe with both hands. *"And people shouldn't post lies,"* she said, pulling the axe back.

The Wizard felt pure panic as he saw the blade hovering over his head, and struggled to pull the remote that Mr. Teller had provided him from his pocket. Just as Dorothy made a move to bring her axe forward he pulled it free and slammed his finger down on the button in the middle of the remote.

For a horrible moment he thought it was too late, but then the ground started to shake around them. There was a whoosh of air as the chair burst out of the tree and moved so quickly toward him it was lifted several inches off the ground. It passed Dorothy and spun her about, temporarily knocking her down and sending her axe flying out of her control. Then the chair circled behind the Wizard and scooped him up.

For a moment he cried *whooo* as the chair snatched him off the ground, and he felt himself being buckled in. The strings above his head hardened to keep the balloons in place, and he felt his hands gripping the arms of the chair. The abrupt jolt jerked him out of the fog he had felt since Dorothy had smashed him.

"What?" Dorothy said, staggering back to her feet. She looked at the chair beneath the Wizard. "What is that?"

"This is Plan B," the Wizard replied. He reached on the right side of the chair, and just as he heard Scarecrow scream (it was getting louder, how could that inferno nuisance be getting *louder*...oh, I did think inferno didn't I, how clever...) he pressed the buttons and several huge gun barrels burst from the side of the chair.

"Oh!" the Wizard said, feeling himself grow a little aroused for the first time in many years. Seeing the fear on Dorothy's face made him even more excited. "Others might not know what these are Dorothy, but being you did spend some time in the United States before coming out here to Oz I'm pretty sure you do."

"I don't remember them ever being so big," Dorothy said, unsure.

The Wizard pulled a trigger. One of the guns exploded in gun fire, bullets flying everywhere and ripping several trees apart, leaving just their trunks behind.

Dorothy's eyes opened in horror. She looked at the axe on the ground but realized she had little chance of getting an attack on the Wizard prior to being torn apart. Especially because the Wizard seemed to be diligently at work aiming the guns at her rather than blindly firing.

She turned and sprinted toward the thickest trees in the grove. Just as she darted behind them the Wizard let loose another barrage of bullets and several of the trees were torn apart. Bullets whizzed by Dorothy's head as she jumped from tree to tree. A few of the trees themselves seemed to be aware they were being used as shields and tried to uproot themselves, to sprint away, but they were too slow, and soon every tree in the grove had been decimated, and Dorothy stood there, shaking and with no shelter.

"Oh there's nowhere to run, Dorothy," the Wizard said joyfully. It indeed was a pleasure to just pull the trigger and hold it down, the bullets destroying everything in their path. Had he had such an invention when he was at the state fair! Why, he could have unloaded on all the people circling about him, on the annoying children clutching at him and his creations. Oh, if only these wonderful inventions had been abound when he was back on Earth, what a glorious world they would make!

Dorothy stood amongst the fallen trees. "Oh please Wizard!" she called out. "We have been through so much together!"

"Yes yes," he replied, placing his finger on the trigger. "But times move on, my child. And our time together is at an end."

Dorothy looked to both sides but with all the trees destroyed there was nowhere to hide. She thought of making a last minute lunge but even as she contemplated how to do this the Wizard's gun extended and the huge barrel was pointed directly at her chest.

She felt a tear escape—one—but she held her chin high.

The Wizard thought he would feel worse than he did. In fact, he was enjoying this all immensely. He watched her for a moment, liking that she knew he had won. *Suck on that, Dorothy!* Finally he started to pull the trigger, thinking he would empty every last bullet into her.

And just then, so loud it was like it was directly in his ear, Scarecrow let loose a ripping scream. And the Wizard realized the scream *was* in his ear as, aflame, Scarecrow threw himself around the Wizard's body and held him tight.

***

SCARECROW HAD THOUGHT ON WHAT HE WOULD DO the night prior (and he was, after all, one of the two best thinkers in all of Oz), and he had decided that no one would ever make him hurt the ones that he loved. And while he had lived in fear of fire since his earliest memory as it was the only thing that could kill him or cause him pain, he felt that the noble gesture of succumbing to fire might be the one thing that would spur the others to resist what they were being forced to do. For if he was willing to burn to death before them, surely nothing Mr. Teller or Mr. Story could do to them could be so bad.

There had been a brief moment after the fire had burnt the life out of him that he felt the peace of nothingness, a womb like acceptance of one's place in the universe...when he suddenly felt his thoughts come back together, first muddled, then clear. And he looked down at his body and realized he was whole again.

Had...had he somehow defeated them? Had this sacrifice been sufficient to drive those horrible people away, to bring he and his friends back to their own world?

And then he had felt the tingling at the tips of his straw fingers again, and a moment later they burst into flames.

The pain had been overwhelming—it had been impossible not to scream. Flames tore through him, and soon he collapsed to ash.

And, he was back. Over and over, he had a moment of consciousness, of awareness, and then he would sense the tingling at his fingers. Then the agonizing pain of the fire tearing through him. Again. And again. And again.

It was during this time that he realized how hard it was to keep his thoughts straight when he was in a cycle of excruciating pain. Even for one of the two best thinkers in the land, it was hard to be productive in the few moments he had between regaining his consciousness and bursting into flames.

He did his best to embrace those frugal moments before he felt the tingle in his fingers, knowing this would be followed with his body engulfed in fire. He thought to himself *I am a martyr, and this is the plight of a martyr.* It gave him some satisfaction but even this was hollow; what was martyrdom when he had accomplished nothing, except extending his own pain.

It was, however, during one of these brief 'martyr' moments that he looked up and across the valley saw Dorothy.

For the shortest of moments he felt some relief. His death was horrible, but if only one of them were to live on at least it would be Dorothy. At least it would be her.

But then he also saw the waddling little troll, that little *egomaniac* with his *giant* head. The Wizard. And Scarecrow saw the look on his face as he emerged from his hidden little tree house which he was so proud of but which Scarecrow had known about from the start. It was a look the Wizard had when he thought all was going his way. When he thought *I have all this under my control.*

Scarecrow did not know why the Wizard thought it, but he clearly felt he would get the best of Dorothy. The smug look on his face said that.

The thought of the Wizard being the last from their home world of Oz was infuriating. He even forgot about his situation for the briefest of moments, until his body burst into flames and he screamed in agony.

But when his body and mind momentarily reformed he had a new determination. It was one thing to think you were a martyr; it was another to make a difference, even when all has been lost.

He started to sprint across the valley, getting as close to the Wizard as he could before his body betrayed him, awash in flame. But when it formed again he gathered himself and continued to run.

For a moment—when he had substantially closed the gap—he thought Dorothy might have gotten the best of the Wizard. This was a relief, as running on burning legs was even worse than just sitting still and waiting for death, somehow. But when he saw Dorothy smash the small screen across the Wizard's head and he stagger back, stunned, Scarecrow thought maybe Dorothy could defeat the Wizard without his help. But when he reformed he was horrified to see what had happened next: the Wizard was now sitting on a chair which had huge guns aimed at Dorothy. He was firing indiscriminately, tearing through all the trees which might serve as shelter for his poor friend.

Scarecrow buckled down and continued to sprint. He ran as fast and as hard as he could, thinking of all the times the

Wizard had put him down, had pointedly said that it was all well and good that Scarecrow's thinking skills had grown, but none compared to his *own* cognitive abilities. Proud of that stupid oversized head of his.

All the trees were gone. The Wizard was pointing his guns at Dorothy. She was doomed but was desperately trying to not show fear. She stood with pride, but pride could not stop bullets. At least not these bullets.

Scarecrow felt the tingling at the tips of his fingers. He did not think he was going to make it. The flames surged through him, the pain overwhelming. But even as his legs started to crumble to dust he lurched forward, throwing his arms around the Wizard and his chair.

The Wizard had been about to pull the trigger and turn Dorothy into an unrecognizable mess, when to his shock he felt the burning straw somehow grabbing him and holding tight.

"*Get...what....GET OFF ME*," he cried, jerking himself forward in the chair, feeling intense heat on his back and shoulders.

Scarecrow tumbled to the ground, burning ash. The Wizard stared, angered and stunned. He tried to lean back in his chair but pain surged through him; he had suffered terrible burns. He tried to get out of his chair but his skin started to pull and tear and he screamed, realizing some of his flesh had been welded to the metal.

A cold fury filled him, but not cold enough to cure his extensive burns. *"You bastard,"* he said, but he was only speaking to a pile of soot…however in front of his eyes it started to re-form.

He backed the chair up, not wanting to deal with Scarecrow when he reappeared. He needed to get some distance between them, and then he could turn his weapons on Dorothy…

Dorothy.

His eyes widened as he realized he had not thought of the girl, and he became aware she was charging at him.

Dorothy's mind had been in turmoil since she had seen that horrible tablet with all the lies that people posted. As the Wizard had leveled his guns at her she had sought some kind of peace; at least it would be over, she thought.

But she did not feel this peace. Death had not come. The Wizard was toying with her. So instead she felt terrified, and angry. She would not show it, though. She would stand her ground and if she went down she would go down on her feet, with her chin pushed out.

She had seen Scarecrow before the Wizard had, though she had been unsure what his intentions were. She then understand and she felt a moment of hope surge through her. But as the flames engulfed Scarecrow she knew he would never make it, he would never actually be able to stop the Wizard from shooting her. But using a will he often showed when thinking hard to solve a problem, Scarecrow lunged his body into the Wizard.

For a delirious moment she was sure the two would burn together, that she would stand over the Wizard's fiery shape with a smile on her face. But, despite sustaining serious injuries, the Wizard was able to shake him off. He began to pat at his own burning flesh, cursing and yelling.

Dorothy stared for longer than she should, but she finally broke the paralysis. She started slow, but then was sprinting, and she was just about to make it to the Wizard when he became aware of her presence.

"*Take this*," the Wizard shouted, and pressed a button on the left arm of his chair.

Dorothy was still approaching him and had planned to tackle him, but at the last moment blades and knives sprung all around the chair, protecting the Wizard and threatening to slice anyone who got too close to his body. Dorothy shifted her trajectory and lost her balance. She started to fly past, grabbing wildly at the back of the chair, a small area which was not protected by sharpened steel.

Dorothy grabbed a knob as she passed and it tore off in her hand. She tumbled to the ground, landing hard on her back.

The Wizard slowly spun his chair. He looked down at her, collapsed on the ground. "You fought, but in the end you fought like a girl," he said. "I had the plan. I had the equipment. You had no chance."

Dorothy clawed backward, staring at the Wizard, who had lost much of his shirt due to the fire, leaving behind bright red and blistering skin.

"One button more and you will be more shis-ka-bob than person," he said smugly, looking to end it.

Dorothy, breathing hard, bleeding and exhausted, held up the knob in her hand.

"What?" the Wizard said, unsure, and then he felt it.

The only part of his chair not covered in knives was the knob attached to the pump that kept his balloons filled with helium.

Dorothy had ripped it free…releasing all the helium at once.

The balloons that kept his head from lolling over soon filled, then expanded more, and more.

Suddenly the balloons were so full they started to pull him off the ground.

"N-no!" he shouted, holding the arms of the chair, and accidentally cutting himself deeply up and down his already blackened wrists.

Dorothy watched as the helium continued pumping into the balloons. He had designed them himself, ensuring they would never burst (it was a technology he had perfected when living in Omaha, which was how the balloon first carried him to Oz) so they just kept getting bigger and bigger, and soon he was several feet off the ground.

"Help me, help me Dorothy!" he called out, reaching down toward her.

Dorothy looked at the outstretched hand and pulled back.

The Wizard's eyes widened in anger. He felt the balloons pulling him higher in the air. He grabbed at a knife on the side of the chair and quickly sliced off two of his fingers. They fell to the ground below, Dorothy deftly side stepping them. The Wizard was finally able to grasp a knife between his thumb and pinky finger and tried to cut at the strings that connected his head to the balloons.

But as Mr. Teller had said, the strings were reinforced so that they could not be cut by an attempted assailant. No matter how hard he cut, the strings stayed firm. His hands were slick with blood and he dropped the knife which fell, blade first, into his own right shoulder.

The Wizard howled in pain, and he and his chair started ascending rapidly into the air. He realized he had no control and no ability to stop as the balloons continued to fill with helium and carry him further upward.

"Dorothy you always were a little bitch," he called as, burned and bleeding, he disappeared into the sky.

***

DOROTHY WALKED IN A DAZE for several moments, aware that while all her friends were now dead, she was still alive.

Alive!

"*Alive!*" she yelled out loud, scurrying some strange insects that had collected at the scent of all the blood that had been spilled. The moment of exhilaration passed as she looked at the ashes of her dear friend Scarecrow. She waited patiently for him to re-form. When he did he focused his attention, trying to ascertain what had happened while he was ash.

"W-where is he? Did we do it?"

"You did it, old friend," Dorothy said. "The Wizard is gone. Thanks to you, he is gone."

Scarecrow had no reply to that, except a smile. He sat down and waited. The flames came, as he knew they would, and while the pain was as vivid, he did not scream this time. He just sat and smiled at Dorothy until he crumbled to dust.

Tears came to Dorothy then, not just for Scarecrow but for all of them. They were all dead, and while this had been an ordeal they had been friends. They had been.

There was little time for grief. In the distance she heard a vibration from under the ground…but then it came closer.

Someone was coming to the surface.

Dorothy found herself walking, and with every step the vibrations beneath the ground grew louder and more intense. She ignored it though…in fact, it was like she didn't even notice.

Instead she walked through the valley, where she saw the fallen body of Lion, who had bled so much the Yellow Brick Road was soaked red. Then she wandered into the grove, where she came upon the partially eaten body of Glinda, and the Hungry Tiger, whose throat had been ripped open.

Her legs continued on and she walked back toward the Emerald City. There she saw the Nome King, some of his guts still hanging from the side of the tower. There was Jack Pumpkinhead, his head exploded and now filled with feeding insects.

She walked to the West. She stood over the frozen body of the Tin Woodman, his head tossed to the side, his body rusted away. Dorothy lingered there, and then she even ascended the stairs of the Wicked Witch's Castle. All the monkeys were gone but what was left of the Witch had been ripped apart and scattered throughout the room.

She exited the tower, and her timing was fortuitous as the ground was shaking so violently that it started to crumble behind her.

She didn't even quicken her pace. She just walked on, and with this fake Oz much tinier than the real had been she was soon back in the valley. Nearby Scarecrow re-formed, screamed in agony, and turned to dust.

The ground shook so violently that twice she fell to one knee. At some point she had reclaimed the Tin Woodman's axe.

Her body had more injuries than she could keep track of but they did not matter. Nothing mattered, anymore.

Soon the whole world was shaking. Then, for the first time, rocks and pebbles at the surface started to spray. Right beneath it, a mighty force pounded against the dirt, sending it flying everywhere. Finally a huge black head emerged from below, sniffing at the air. A scent was caught and he started to growl, turning his giant head toward Dorothy as he pulled the rest of his body from the soil.

"Hello Toto," Dorothy said.

***

WHEN TOTO FIRST ENTERED THE LAND OF OZ he discovered a horrible, horrible thing. While back in Kansas his mind was full of wonderful images— Dorothy, belly rubs, a dog bowl filled with scraps of meats, even the big shiny ball in the sky that warmed his fur and made him fall into wonderful, lazy naps—suddenly his thoughts were made up of these horrible *words*.

In Kansas his thoughts were occasionally punctuated by words. He recognized *Toto* and *treat* and *dinner*. But now words played with his mind every day, and as he saw creatures around him chatting away he realized he too had the ability to have these conversations.

173

And worse Dorothy, whom he loved with all his tiny but mighty terrier heart, encouraged him to speak.

Come now Toto, how come all the animals speak here but you?

He refused and he refused until the weight of it started to build on him. And one day when he woke up he realized his belly was a tad higher off the ground, his snout thicker. His teeth bigger.

Dorothy noticed and marveled at the magic of Oz…and encouraged him to speak on it.

Come Toto, you are bigger! Surely you have something to say on the matter. All the other creatures in Oz are talking about it, why shouldn't you?

But he swallowed these words and tried to repress the thoughts that now bombarded him constantly. While in the past gentle images of cats and squirrels running through the farm accompanied him to sleep, now he closed his eyes and these horrible horrible *thoughts* would not leave him alone. Why had he come here? Why couldn't he go back? What happens when you die? Why did Dorothy insist he talk? What would she taste like?

He would groan in his sleep and then howl at the pain as he felt his frustrations settle in his stomach, his bones, his muscles. He would wake up larger than when he had gone to bed and Dorothy would again marvel at it, and instead of giving him space (or perhaps querying on whether he liked these changes) would ask questions and encourage him to talk, setting the cycle in motion all over again.

In addition to his body, quite naturally his hunger began to grow. This had not occurred to Dorothy, who continued to feed him dog treats and biscuits she had carried from Kansas, with no thought to his additional girth.

Toto had started sneaking away at night and hunting. The creatures he slayed would cry out and call for help, and inevitably he was caught feasting on an animal whose family had come out demanding retribution.

Toto had been acting out of hunger, not malice, and he thought this should excuse his actions. But when Dorothy came out and said *Toto! How could you?* he had felt an intense shame. For just because he hated his life here, and just because he hated himself and all the horrible words that harassed him every moment, he still loved Dorothy. Loved her as much as he used to when they were in Kansas together and they would walk through the fields and he would bark at animals and have no nagging thoughts bothering him.

His frustration grew so overwhelming that he became a giant animal, much larger than Lion, than the Hungry Tiger, than any four legged beast in Oz. To deal with his shame (and his hunger) he burrowed into the ground, dug out tunnels (many of these had been prepared by the Nome King, who had a kingdom beneath the surface, but Toto made them much bigger and wider). He would find underworld creatures, and even as they were introducing themselves he would gobble them in one bite. Soon he had become a menace to the tunnels and the world below the surface; his giant steps meant doom for any not fast enough to get out of his way.

He stayed down for what felt like eternity. He was overwhelmed with loneliness, and the only solace he ever found was in dreams, when sometimes those words abandoned him, and he lived in a world of images, in a time when he and Dorothy were together, in a place that no longer existed for him.

He would have stayed in the tunnels forever, but just as Mr. Teller and Mr. Story had visited the others they had planted the seed in Toto as well.

He had woken from an uneasy sleep to find the two men standing before him. One wore a mask with a checkered pattern on it and two black eyes. The other wore no mask but gazed at him impassively.

A growl had built in his throat.

Enough Mr. Teller said, and suddenly Toto felt a shock in his testicles that made him howl in pain. He looked at the men with large, hurt eyes.

Now that we have your attention Mr. Teller said.

Toto remained at alert, fur taut, teeth exposed. But he was on his hind legs, looking to flee and not attack.

You can growl and bark and drool all you want Mr. Teller said coldly. *But I know you are well aware of every word being uttered.*

In one day's time you are to surface. If you encounter any beings you should kill them, because if you don't they will kill you. Do you understand?

Toto's only response was a deep growl.

Mr. Story leaned forward and whispered in Mr. Teller's ear.

Mr. Teller nodded. *I assume you understand and you will comply. Or you will feel a great deal of pain.* He leveled a look from the top of his long nose at Toto, expecting him to whimper or show some submission.

But Toto did not. He just stood there, taut, a deep growl in his throat.

Oh you're just a bloody dog Mr. Teller said, and sent an even larger shock through the beast's genitalia.

Toto held his ground for a moment, but then threw his body against the side of the tunnel, howling.

Some rocks trickled down on them, and a well placed one hit the arm of Mr. Story and his quill pen tumbled from his hand to the ground.

Brother! shouted Mr. Teller, his voice filled with panic.

Toto sensed it but was too busy dealing with the roiling pain spreading through his body to do anything. By the time he looked up, the excruciating pain now settled to a distant throb, Mr. Story had his quill back, and the two of them were gone.

Toto had spent the hours that followed in a waking nightmare, storming through the tunnels and decimating any creature foolish enough to cross his path. Every time he closed his eyes to sleep he was riddled with horrible words, the worst of which being the ones spoken to him by Mr. Teller.

Yes, he was more consumed with rage than anything else. But by staying under the ground he did not see those who used to be his companions. Now when he closed his eyes even when he was able to see images they were of Dorothy, ripped to pieces, or he tearing flesh from Lion, or shredding Scarecrow.

As time passed Toto became aware of the violence and bloodshed occurring on the surface. The smell of blood seeped into the ground and both saddened him and filled his mouth with hot saliva. He desperately tried to stay under the surface but as more and more time passed he started feeling that horrible pain again and he realized that it wasn't coincidental; those nasty people were tweaking his pain, making sure he understood what would happen if he didn't cooperate.

If he didn't go to the surface.

It finally reached a point where it became unbearable. The smell of blood, the constant small jolts being sent through him, those horrible *thoughts*…he was enraged to the point that he started to scratch diligently at the ground above his head, thrusting himself forward until finally he punched his huge front paws through the grassy terrain. Then he pushed his enormous head through, snarling as his mouth filled with dry dirt. He pushed his two front paws over the surface, blinking at the bright sun in his face. It was only as he wriggled the rest of his huge body out of the ground that he was able to orient himself to the brightness and to what was happening around him.

The valley he found himself was filled with blood and the smell of smoke.

And standing across from him, holding a sharpened axe, was Dorothy.

His Dorothy.

Despite this he felt a growl build in his throat. He knew what he was supposed to do. And the smell of blood, the brightness of the world, the pain that riddled his body made it impossible to think of any other options.

"Hello Toto," Dorothy called out.

Toto stepped forward. He was surrounded with the rancid and sweet smell of blood curdling in the sun.

"*Stay back*," Dorothy said, swinging the axe in front of her. Her eyes desperately flitted about, looking for a weakness in the giant beast as Toto continued on her, his legs lowered to the ground, his teeth bared.

The little armor that Dorothy had been provided had been ripped free and hung in tatters from long before. Even with it, Dorothy knew it would have no chance against the enormous teeth exposed before her. Lion had seemed huge when he had been attacking her, but nothing like Toto, who was twice his size.

Dorothy feinted at Toto, then swung the axe.

Toto hardly even flinched. He started to circle around Dorothy, and she was soon backing up on the grass, swinging the axe back and forth in front of her.

"*Stay back,*" Dorothy yelled, hysteria in her voice. She swung the blade again and lost her balance in a puddle of congealed blood and fell down to one knee. Toto rushed her, snapping at her arm. She yanked back, then landed on her rear, Toto towering over her.

Dorothy was bathed in a thick slobber that poured down on her head. She used her left hand to wipe the saliva from her forehead, then looked up through smeared eyes and yelled out, "*Bad dog Toto!*"

For one moment Toto's eyes widened in surprise, but then they narrowed as he bared his teeth once again.

Dorothy pushed herself back to her feet. She pointed an index finger at Toto and waggled it at him, much as she had when Toto barely made it to her ankles and he had made a puddle on the rug in Auntie Em's house.

"*You are being a very bad dog, Toto!*" she said sharply.

Toto was still for a moment, then his giant teeth disappeared within his giant mouth. His eyes opened a little wider, but then he lowered them, as if ashamed. A small whimper escaped his throat.

"Oh Toto," Dorothy said, and she stepped forward. Just then she heard the sound of something large rushing at her from above. She looked up and could barely get a scream out.

The Wizard's chair had risen higher and higher in the air. The chair that had been given him as a gift he realized would be his downfall. The knives and blades would not withdraw, the helium kept pouring into the balloons, and his badly burned body was welded into the chair so that even pulling free a bit was tearing his skin right off, flaying him in mid-air. He had been trying to reach around the back to adjust the helium but his partially melted skin was not cooperating. Finally, with one great yank he had pulled much of the skin off his lower back and he started to jam his thumb where the knob had been.

Just turn it, just turn it he thought, but instead he seemed to press some sort of fail safe that cut off *all* helium to the balloons. In fact, above him he could hear the balloons start to rapidly decrease, the helium being released into the air.

"No, no, *no*," he said, and then the chair started to plummet. He screamed as the ground rushed at him ridiculously fast.

The blade covered chair came down directly through the head and much of the neck of the giant dog. The Wizard was flung from the chair (ripping off a great deal more skin) and he skidded across the ground at an exorbitant speed, snapping his spine in seventeen places and breaking his neck so badly his giant head just rolled off his body.

Dorothy was knocked off her feet, dazed, a sharp pain on her left side. She lay on the ground, breathing hard, trying to orient herself. She heard the sound of whimpering, of pain. She managed to pull herself back up.

Toto was lying on his side. Half his head was caved in, much of the right side of his face, now facing the sky, had been sheared off. He was still alive, barely. He whimpered, blood dribbling from his mouth.

"Toto," Dorothy said, too stunned to be aware of her own injuries. She moved to him. "Toto," she said miserably.

Toto's eyes rolled up to her and for one time, the last time, his giant tail gave a thump, going up and down. His lips were quivering and he made a slight whistling sound.

"Toto?" Dorothy said, leaning in. "Toto?"

"D-D-Dorothy," Toto whispered.

"Hey boy," she said. She had never heard him speak before.

"I n-n-never…wanted to be…a bad boy," he whispered, then his body grew taut as a spasm of pain shot through him. He almost lifted off the ground, but when it passed he collapsed down, his eyes rolled up, his tongue lolled out.

"*Toto*," Dorothy cried out. She tried to put her arms around him, to hold his misshapen, giant head, and it was only then that she realized she had no control over her left arm.

She was able to turn her head and she saw why. She had mostly avoided the blades…but not completely. Her left arm had almost been cut clean off, with just a strand of muscle in her upper arm keeping it dangling below. Blood poured down, and she realized she was already feeling light headed.

She managed to get to her feet and staggered away from Toto. She walked in a bit of a circle, surveying Oz (even if it was an imitation) for the last time. Then she looked to the sky.

"Are you...are you watching?" she said. "You must...be happy. No one...no one left..." She wanted to say something else, something profound. But she still felt all her blood pouring from her severed arm, and she barely was able to say, "I am...Dorothy," before she collapsed to the ground, waiting to bleed out.

***

MR. TELLER AND MR. STORY WERE

INDEED HAPPY. The two of them walked through the landscape of the Oz they had created, surveying all. Behind them several wolves (walking on two legs, not four) followed, waiting for directions.

"So if they are all dead all rules were abided by," Mr. Teller was saying, quite enthusiastically. "That is one less remnant of this...place. It ends them that much sooner."

Mr. Story, however, detected something. And when he pointed it out, Mr. Teller was definitively *not* happy.

"How…how could that be?" he said. He walked quickly across the valley, kicking through the final ash of Scarecrow, who was no longer regenerating just to combust again. He bent down to Dorothy, sprawled across the blood soaked ground, her left arm pulled free from her body.

He placed his hand against Dorothy's neck. And while the pulse was faint, it was there.

"*How*," he demanded.

Mr. Story then raised a hand and pointed to the blood around Dorothy's side. While indeed there was a great deal, he indicated there should have been more. He also pointed to the wound on Dorothy's arm.

Mr. Teller was one to grow agitated and he felt that now. The wolves who had been trailing scattered a bit, familiar with his temper. He pointed to the sky. "*Show me what happened*," he shouted.

Dorothy, lying at their feet, was dazed, in and out of fantasies and dreams and nightmares. The last one was the worst of all because she was feeling pain. How could one feel pain in dreams? And, as bad, those two horrible figures—Mr. Teller and Mr. Story—were hovering over her, speaking softly. She could hear what Mr. Teller said clearly, but everything Mr. Story said was muffled through the cloth he wore over his face.

It was only when she heard the sound of the giant screen lowering from the sky that she realized this was no longer a dream or a nightmare or a fantasy. And as much as she might wish she could feel the relief of death, she was very much alive.

"*Show me,*" Mr. Teller called to the sky.

Dorothy managed to just open one eye. Once it adjusted to the light she was able to see the screen.

To her horror the first thing she saw was herself. She was holding onto Toto's giant head, her little sweet dog who had been turned into a monster by Oz. She heard Toto say, just before death took him, *I never wanted to be a bad dog* and she shook her head ever so slightly because Toto had always been a good dog, he had always protected her, he had always wanted nothing more than to be by her side…till they came to Oz, of course. Till the change.

Dorothy watched as she staggered away from the fallen bladed chair, away from her big dead dog. Her left arm had been ripped practically clean off and blood sprayed everywhere.

I will bleed out she thought, watching the thick stream hit the ground with such force it splashed back up. *No way I could survive.*

But then she—and her two captors—saw as Scarecrow lurched one final time to her.

Scarecrow had known this was it. As evil as Mr. Story and Mr. Teller were, they set up rules and they abided by those rules. He would continue to go through this horrible cycle of being re-formed only to burn to death until the game was over, until there was only one left in Oz. And Dorothy was that one.

But not for long. He watched as Dorothy collapsed to the ground, sure she would bleed out even as he burst into flames for the last time. He thought quickly (and after all, he was the second best thinker in Oz…although with the Wizard's mangled body clearly lifeless he assumed he was *the* best thinker in Oz now, har dee har har). His hands and arms had already been burnt away, so he leaned forward and pressed his head at the spot blood pulsated out. Dorothy twitched as the fire cauterized the wound, but she remained unconscious on the ground. Scarecrow, through his flames, managed to stay focused long enough to see the deed was done. Then, despite the pain, he was able to sit down with some relief, and burn until he was no more than ash, not to be brought back again.

"*Damn it,*" Mr. Teller exclaimed, looking about for the dust that had once been Scarecrow. Could he be punished again? Could dust be punished? Finally he just sighed. "I guess she will pass into the next round."

Mr. Story reached forward and whispered in his ear. Then he pulled his quill out.

"*What?*" demanded Mr. Teller. "Are you sure? It could cause her to live on and…"

Mr. Story interrupted with a sharp jab at his ribs.

"Ouch. Don't be cruel." Mr. Teller sighed. "Fine. If you think that is for the best Br…"

And then Mr. Story spoke again, his voice just loud enough for Dorothy to actually hear the words.

"I thinks she is awake," he said.

"What? Can't be." Mr. Teller bent down so his face was right in Dorothy's; his long nose almost reached her own.

Dorothy was still but then she flinched, the unpleasant smell from his breath bearing down on her.

"Why yes, she is. Dorothy? Come girl, I know you hear me."

Dorothy had hoped to feign death (or at least unconsciousness) until the two of them left, but reluctantly opened her eyes.

Mr. Teller surprised her with a smile. "You won, my girl. *This* round, at least. And perhaps we can help out because this…" he gave a small kick at the stub that hung from her right shoulder, causing her to flinch in pain. "This will do no good at all."

Dorothy tried to speak but her lips were dry and bloodless.

"Tut tut," Mr. Teller said. "Your adventure is just beginning. And as for Oz…it will never be heard from again."

Dorothy wanted to speak up and tell him that he was wrong on both counts. That indeed her adventure was *done* and she would never do this again, and surely the real Oz was out there and stories were taking place there and magic was happening there, even as she lay bloodied at his feet. But before she could get a word out she watched as Mr. Story jotted something down with his quill pen and she felt consciousness slip quickly away.

***

"IS YOUR NAME DOROTHY?"

Dorothy had been in a dreamless sleep, and she opened her eyes, trying to orient herself.

There was a large face looking down at her, an unfamiliar face. It was a small horse—no, a donkey, just like they used to have on Auntie Em's farm. Of course those donkeys had slow and stupid eyes and didn't speak, but since her time at Oz Dorothy was quite familiar with animals who should not be speaking having an extensive vocabulary.

"Is your name Dorothy?" the donkey asked again, his voice slow and dulled.

Dorothy tried to sit, but was stunned by how heavy her left arm felt. She pushed herself up and realized she was resting on a plush, thick chair with satin lining. It was indeed luxurious, but she could not focus on that, not with the donkey still looking at her, and with the strange heaviness coming from her left side.

"Why yes," she said, trying to sound pert. "I am Dorothy."

"That's good. That's really good. I like Dorothy." Every word was spoken with a dull slur, weighed down. "My name is Eeyore. I want us to be friends."

Dorothy had a vague memory of Eeyore, of seeing him on the giant screen when they had watched the creatures from the 100 Acre Wood in their own horrible battle to the death. She would have sworn she and her friends from Oz would never resort to anything like that.

She felt tears fill her eyes and she went to wipe them away—and for the first time found herself moving her left arm. It toggled a bit, out of control, and she stared at it in shock.

"Why will you look at that," Eeyore said. "An arm made of metal. I have never seen an arm that looked like that."

Dorothy stared at it in awe. "Tin," she said softly, it dawning on her that they had removed her butchered limb and replaced it with the Tin Woodman's arm. Staring at it she managed to open and close her tin fist.

There was a small table next to her chair and on it was a thick bronze cup. It took some heavy concentration, but she was able to pick up the cup and with one ounce of pressure crush it. "Groovy," she said.

"Well look at that. You squashed the cup. No more cup."

Dorothy looked about herself; she was in a huge room, like one would see in a mansion. There was no one in the room besides her and Eeyore.

Her sadness was temporarily blinked away, replaced with hope…and anger.

Mr. Teller and Mr. Story will pay, she thought. She did not know how…yet.

But they would.

Eeyore was still looking at her with a glum sort of face so she reached forward with her right, flesh hand, and rubbed him behind his ears.

"We will be friends, Eeyore. We will be the best of friends."

"Oh good, I like friends," Eeyore replied and stood in silence.

This was okay with Dorothy. She had a lot to think about.

The tale continues Christmas, 2022 with *Chattel Royale 2: Monsters*, because what better way to celebrate the holiday season than to see Count Dracula, Dr. Frankenstein and his Monster, the Invisible Man, Dr. Jekyll and Mr. Hyde, and many more ripping each other to pieces.